What the press says about Harlequin Romances…

"…clean, wholesome fiction…always with an upbeat, happy ending."
— *San Francisco Chronicle*

"…a work of art."
— *The Globe & Mail*, Toronto

"Nothing quite like it has happened since *Gone With the Wind*…"
— *Los Angeles Times*

"…among the top ten…"
— *International Herald-Tribune*, Paris

"Women have come to trust these clean, easy-to-read love stories about contemporary people, set in exciting foreign places."
— *Best Sellers*, New York

OTHER
Harlequin Romances
by LUCY GILLEN

Many of these titles are available at your local bookseller
or through the Harlequin Reader Service.

For a free catalogue listing all available Harlequin Romances,
send your name and address to:

HARLEQUIN READER SERVICE,
M.P.O. Box 707, Niagara Falls, N.Y. 14302
Canadian address: Stratford, Ontario, Canada N5A 6W2

or use order coupon at back of book.

Back of Beyond

by

LUCY GILLEN

Harlequin Books

TORONTO • LONDON • NEW YORK • AMSTERDAM • SYDNEY

Original hardcover edition published in 1978
by Mills & Boon Limited

ISBN 0-373-02178-X

Harlequin edition published July 1978

CHAPTER ONE

FERN SUTTON was used to looking after herself. In her home town in the south Midlands she had had her own flat and managed her home as efficiently as she managed her job as secretary. She was, after all, twenty-four years old since last month, and she had been running her own life since she was little more than seventeen, when her mother died.

Soon after the death of her mother the family house had been sold and her father moved into a small, modern maisonette which was much nearer to his place of work, and which he ran with the help of a part-time housekeeper. Fern had relished her independence, but not so her father, for only six months afterwards his part-time housekeeper had become Fern's step-mother. Not that Fern blamed him too much, for her father was not nearly as capable of coping alone as he thought, and his second wife was a pleasant and companionable enough woman.

The move to Lincolnshire had been an impulsive one on Fern's part, and not really like her, but she had decided that a change would be a good thing. It was time she tried somewhere different, and left the town she had known all her life. A job as secretary to an estate manager in the Lincolnshire fens had been advertised in her local newspaper, and it sounded different enough to interest her.

Her reply had been answered promptly, suggesting that the interview take place at an hotel in a nearby town, Thorpe St Mary being not very accessible by public transport. That was a month ago, and the whole matter had been completed so quickly and so easily that she still had difficulty believing it had happened.

Roy Barton, her prospective employer, had impressed her, even though he rather gave Fern the impression that he was not really at home in the atmosphere of a city hotel. Fern was, he had confessed, the only applicant for the job; apparently few young women were prepared to bury themselves in the wilds of the Lincolnshire countryside. In fact Fern herself admitted to certain qualms when she heard it described as such.

She had not yet actually seen Thorpe St Mary itself, but it sounded a pleasant enough location as described by Roy Barton; a little isolated, perhaps, but that was no more than she would expect in fen country. The sea was quite close by, and a small cottage on the estate went with the job. It was the thought of having her own cottage in the country that really swung the balance, for the idea was irresistible to someone like Fern, born and bred in a large industrial town.

Until she arrived at Sandmere Halt she had been pretty optimistic, but she knew that from here on there were no more trains, and she arrived in time to learn that the four-times-daily bus had already left. It was not an auspicious start, but for the moment she did not let it trouble her too much.

Sandmere Halt, in fact, seemed to be nothing more than a couple of brick-built huts and a few yards of concrete platform put up in the middle of nowhere, for she could see no other sign of habitation, only a pile of boxes apparently containing produce from some farm in the neighbourhood. The only human being other than herself was an elderly and lugubrious-looking character who was apparently all the staff that Sandmere Halt possessed. To make matters worse it was pouring with rain when she arrived.

She could ring for a taxi, the elderly character informed her, if she had a mind to; that would take her out to Thorpe St Mary and Barton's Fen. In fact seeing that the bus would take her only as far as the end of the private road, a taxi was probably a better idea. It was a fact that had evidently not occurred to him before, for he mused on it for some time while Fern made up her mind.

She begged change from the till in his little ticket office, and rang a number that she found scribbled in Biro on the wall of the telephone kiosk, giving the name of a local taxi driver. The woman who answered seemed in some doubt as to just how long it would be before her husband returned from his last trip, but she would tell him as soon as he came in, she promised, and she seemed so anxious to oblige that Fern hadn't the heart to tell her not to bother, she would ring someone else—if indeed there was anyone else.

Sandmere Halt did not boast a waiting-room, so Fern stood under the picot-edged overhang of the station roof and pondered on the first drawback of isolation. Her suitcases beside her, she watched the road both ways because she had no idea from which direction the taxi would be coming, nor in which direction it would take her when it did arrive. With the outlook as it was, she preferred not to speculate on which desolate, windswept panorama her new home was situated in.

Being preoccupied, she was completely unaware of the occasional searching look she received through the small trapdoor window of the ticket office. The elderly man watched her appraisingly and not unappreciatively for all his advancing years, for Fern was a girl who was worthy of anyone's second look.

She was dark, with a small neat figure and almost black hair. Huge eyes, set between thick dark lashes, were an intriguing mixture of hazel with warming gold

flecks in their depths, and she would need to spend
quite some time in the country air before she lost that
very light creamy skin that showed how much of her
life had been spent living in a town. Her mouth was
full and soft and, at the moment, slightly downturned
because she felt lost and rather disturbingly vulnerable
—a completely new sensation for her.

She had put on a dark blue crimplene suit to travel
in, but she had no raincoat or topcoat and nothing on
her head, so that she was stranded until the taxi came
for her, and she was growing impatient. One neatly
shod foot tapped, almost unconsciously, on the concrete platform, and the station staff noticed it and
shook his head. Town folks never had enough patience!

In company with Fern, he turned his head at the
sound of an approaching car along the narrow, waterlogged road, but whereas the man in the ticket-office
shook his head, Fern stepped quickly forward from the
shelter of the wooden awning and was lifting her suitcases into the back of the vehicle almost before it had
stopped.

'I thought you were never coming,' she told the man,
who turned and grinned at her over his shoulder while
she brushed a few stray drops of rain from the shoulders
of her jacket. 'I have to get to Barton's Fen, please. It's
near Thorpe St Mary, do you know where I mean?'

He wasn't wearing a cap and for some reason Fern
registered the fact that he had thick fair hair that grew
as far as the collar of the bright blue shirt he was wearing. He was still smiling when he reached back and
slammed the door, then he touched his brow with a
forefinger and started the car moving again.

'Yes, *ma'am*!'

There was something about him that did not quite
fit in with her idea of what a taxi driver should be, but
Fern was too preoccupied and too glad to see him to be

too critical, and she sat back in the deep, comfortable seat and sighed her relief. In the pouring rain the countryside was hardly inspiring, but it would not be fair to judge anywhere in the present conditions, and at least she was dry and comfortable and on her way to her new home and job.

The road was narrow and wound its way in tortuous twists and turns between wide ditches that sprouted tall feather-headed reeds which the wind bowed and whipped almost to ground level. The blustering half-gale, she guessed, was coming in off the North Sea, for by studying a large-scale map of the area she had discovered that Thorpe St Mary was little more than a hamlet, lying close to the sea and near a ragged inlet of water shown on the map as Mere Creek.

Beyond the reed-filled ditches, which she hastily re-called were known as dykes in this part of the world, were fields where cattle and sheep huddled against the biting wind in bovine resignation. For not only was the country completely flat, it was virtually devoid of trees and hedges, except for a couple of bulky may trees that stood half-way down one side of a field. In fact to Fern at the moment it appeared alarmingly bleak and inhospitable, although she did her best not to let herself become too discouraged. When the rain stopped and the sun shone it was probably quite different.

It occurred to her suddenly that they seemed to have been going for quite a long time, and the matter of the fare began to concern her; maybe she had been rash to simply order a taxi without finding out just what it was likely to cost her. After all, there was another bus later in the day and she could have waited for that, she supposed.

She looked around the comfortable interior of the car for a meter to give her some idea of what it had cost her so far, but she failed to find one and frowned, only half-conscious of being watched by way of the driving mirror. A carrier bag stood on the other end of the seat from her, looking somehow rather incongruous in such a large and luxurious car with such down-to-earth things as cornflakes, butter and eggs poking out of it.

Presumably the driver had been doing some shopping for his wife, but it seemed curious that he had brought it with him when he came out again, instead of leaving it with her. Looking at the back of the driver's head for a moment, Fern felt suddenly and inexplicably un-easy, and as she looked away she caught sight of a tanned and smiling face in the driving mirror. A pair of bright, gleaming blue eyes held her gaze for a second, then one lid was lowered briefly in a broad and un-mistakable wink.

Startled and vaguely disturbed, she stared out of the streaming windows when she realised that they had turned suddenly on to an even narrower track, and Fern hung on grimly as they bumped over the ruts while mud and water flew up on either side of them. She had a brief glimpse of a board tacked to a solitary chest-nut tree that gave shelter to two small brick cottages, but it was gone before she had time to see more than the word Fen—her new home was number two Fen Cottages.

'I don't see a meter,' she ventured, her voice jerky and breathless as she clung to the handle on the door and, catching that bright gaze on her once more, she hastened to explain. 'We seem to have come rather a long way and——'

'About a couple of miles,' the driver informed her, trying to catch her eye again, and Fern noticed rather absently that he seemed to have an accent of some kind. American, she thought, or possibly Canadian, she wasn't very good at distinguishing one from the other at first. 'This is it—Barton's Fen.'

Fern pondered for a moment on the prospect of the acres of sodden countryside that lay between her and the nearest link with civilisation, and she experienced her first real tremor of doubt. 'I hadn't quite realised how far it was,' she ventured.

The blue eyes managed to catch and hold her uncertain gaze and the rather lopsided grin that accompanied the scrutiny seemed curiously comforting somehow. 'You do want to go to the house, I guess?'

The accent was definitely Canadian, Fern decided, but she felt a lot less certain about her destination. She hadn't really thought what her first move should be, but since her new employer was also to be her landlord and would be almost certain to have the key to her cottage, she supposed she would have to see him first.

Whatever happened, it was too late to have second thoughts about anything now. She was committed to a month at Barton's Fen and she must make the best of it, even if she scuttled off back to city life immediately the trial period was over. She hastily avoided looking at the driver again, and clenched her hands tightly over the clasp of her handbag.

'I'd better call at the house first——' She hesitated, vaguely irritated by her own uncharacteristic nervousness. 'I don't know how long I shall be, but as it's still raining, would you mind waiting until I've seen Mr Barton?' She glanced back along the muddy track and shuddered. Expense or not, she could not face walking back along there carrying her suitcases, and she could not be absolutely sure that Roy Barton would provide an alternative. 'Those cottages back there—they were Fen Cottages, weren't they?'

'That's right, honey—numbers one and two!'

Fern was not accustomed to being addressed as honey,

and she frowned instinctively at the irrepressible grin reflected in the driving mirror. 'On second thoughts,' she told him with a hint of coolness in her voice, 'perhaps I'd better pay you off and make some other arrangements.'

'It's your tune, honey, you whistle it!'

The grin was once more in evidence as he swung the big car round a sudden sharp bend and pulled up in front of a house that seemed to have suddenly appeared out of nowhere in the misty drizzle that the downpour had been reduced to. In such conditions Barton's Fen could hardly have been called welcoming, although Fern suspected that it would look much different in better circumstances.

A gravel drive curved round in front of it, overgrown in places with thick shrubs that drooped in the rain and gave a dismal aspect to her first sight of it. It was built of red brick and its front elevation had the curious arched appearance that Fern always thought of as Dutch; a low porch projected from the front, making a single dark aperture in the flat-faced look of it, and the windows were tall and narrow.

'You're quite sure I shouldn't wait?'

The driver was out of his seat, shirt collar turned up against the rain as he came round to open the door for her, and he reached in for her suitcases with one hand while the other was extended to offer assistance as she got out. Glancing up at the tall blank windows, Fern shook her head.

'No, it's all right, thank you. I'm sure Mr Barton will make certain I don't have to walk back in the rain.'

'Oh, I'm sure of it, too!'

He had stepped back so that he stood just under the edge of the porch roof, but he still caught some of the drizzling mist as it swept in on the wind, the seemingly inevitable grin crinkling his eyes and sending fine lines darting from their corners, like a fine web of laughter in the tanned face.

It was impossible for Fern to miss the implication and she angled her chin in a way that was equally unmistakable. That and the look in the gold-flecked hazel eyes sought to put him firmly in his place, although she had the uncomfortable feeling that it was something more easily said than done.

'If you'll let me know how much I owe you,' she said in her coolest secretarial voice, and he laughed.

'Forget it, honey, you don't owe me a thing!' Fern stared at him, and he shook his head. 'I was coming this way anyway, so a few more yards didn't hurt.'

For the first time Fern took a really good look at the car she had ridden in, and the awful truth began to dawn on her as soon as she noticed the absence of either a taxi sign or the unmistakable yellow licence plates. She wasn't given to blushing as a rule, but she could feel the colour flooding into her face when she realised, and knew that bright, amused gaze was still fixed on her.

It was still drizzling and the wind beat it in under the sheltering porch, whipping it against them, but Fern almost blessed its cool chill on her burning cheeks as she stood there and tried to find words. She had never felt more foolish in her life before, and the fact that the man whose car she had more or less commandeered was smiling as if he found the whole thing vastly amusing only made matters worse. It was so much more difficult to apologise when he was so obviously laughing at her and, carefully avoiding his eyes, she reached and took her suitcases from him, feeling herself actually tremble with embarrassment.

'If you'd pointed out my mistake in the very beginning,' she told him, 'this wouldn't have happened.'

'Honey, if you'd given me time to say anything at all,

I might have! I stopped to give you a lift if I could, and you took it for granted I was Tom Maynard's taxi, so why should I disillusion you?'

'Because you could have saved me a great deal of embarrassment!'

He was getting quite wet and the shirt across his back was soaked to a darker blue and clung to the broad tanned shoulders beneath it, but he seemed oblivious to any discomfort as he ran a hand through his darkening fair hair and shook his head. 'Why make a big deal of it, honey? I gave a neighbour a lift, that's all. No call to go making a big event of it, it's all quite respectable.' A large hand was thrust upon her notice, and she registered vaguely how long and strong the brown fingers were that closed around hers when she responded involuntarily to the gesture. 'My name's Scott Redman—I have the cottage next to yours.'

'Fern Sutton.'

She gave him her name automatically, her self-confidence not yet fully recovered, and Scott Redman was regarding her still with a bright-eyed boldness that she found incredibly discomfiting in the circumstances. Heaven knew what he thought her motive had been in taking his fortuitous appearance for granted, but she found it even more discomfiting to think of him as her neighbour. Those little cottages huddled beneath the chestnut tree had looked very close together, and the drawbacks to living and working at Barton's Fen became increasingly evident with every minute. Maybe even her new employer would prove less amiable than her first impression of him.

'You won't mind having me for a neighbour, will you?' he asked, and Fern did not bother to reply.

Instead she hefted her suitcase in either hand and turned to face a plain wooden door that stood in virtual darkness under the porch. It did not suggest a very warm welcome and Scott Redman, whoever he might be apart from her next-door neighbour, was cheerful. She had not yet thanked him either, she recalled, and set about remedying the fact. Turning back to him, she tried a half-smile that betrayed the way she felt, possibly more obviously than she realised.

'I'm sorry about this—this whole thing, Mr Redman, but I was in such a hurry to get here that I didn't really look to make sure I was getting into a taxi. In the circumstances it was very good of you to bring me and——'

'I told you, forget it, honey!' He glanced at the closed door, standing with both hands thrust into the front pockets of his slacks. 'I guess Roy Barton will give you a cuppa, so I won't bother putting on the kettle, but if you feel like borrowing a hefty shoulder when you move in, just bang on the wall!'

Things were going just a bit too fast for Fern to do any more than nod and smile vaguely at him. As it happened there was no time for her to do anything else, because the door behind them opened suddenly and a woman stood in the doorway. She looked first at Scott Redman and then at Fern, and frowned.

'I presume you're Miss Sutton, are you?'

From the tone of voice Fern would have concluded that this was Mrs Roy Barton, if he had not already told her that he was a single man. The woman, whoever she was, gave the impression that she was in charge and had every right to address her in that short, peremptory tone, and the effect was to make Fern suspicious.

'I'm Fern Sutton,' she started to say, but before she could speak for herself the man beside her stepped in quickly.

The gleam in his eyes looked faintly malicious and the deep and very masculine voice assumed a slow drawl that made it sound much more transatlantic, so that Fern felt sure he was enjoying the situation as much as he had her earlier discomfiture. 'Miss Sutton, this is Frances Dean, your boss's housekeeper—*Mrs* Dean.'

'Please come inside, Miss Sutton.'

Her companion was rather pointedly ignored and Fern glanced at him instinctively before she stepped inside the house. Maybe the offhand coolness of the reception was aimed only at Scott Redman, but somehow Fern felt that chilly atmosphere was meant to include her too, and it was hardly encouraging. Turning in the doorway, she half-smiled to let him know that she appreciated what he had done for her.

'Thank you again, Mr Redman, and I'm sorry about —the mistake.'

'Think nothing of it!' A casual hand both dismissed her thanks and served as a farewell salute, and he ducked back into the car while Mrs Dean was still closing the door. 'See you!'

The hall wasn't as big as Fern would have expected in a house of this size, and it was much too gloomy for her own taste, although almost certainly the weather had something to do with that too. The floor was laid with black and white tiles, with only an occasional rug to relieve the stark chilliness of it, and the walls were half-panelled in dark oak with a white wash above.

A wide straight staircase rose from the right-hand side and was also panelled in oak and lit by a window at the top, the carpet on the treads a deep warm red. It could, Fern guessed, have been a rather attractive introduction to the house if more attention had been given to comfort; but then Barton's Fen was primarily a functional farm house and the home of a bachelor.

The housekeeper seemed rather young for her post, if one took the traditional view of housekeepers, although her own father's choice had been even younger. The woman was tall and her colouring was of a nondescript mixture of browns, hair and eyes too, even her complexion. She was well-built and the cotton dress she wore with a light wool cardigan showed off quite a good figure, but Fern suspected that she seldom smiled, for the tight mouth had not even twitched when she met her, and it was tight set now as Fern followed her across the hall.

A light rap on one of the doors was all she did before walking in without waiting for a reply, and Fern, following her still, felt her heart beating just a little more anxiously as she walked into what was obviously an office. It was a big room and would perhaps be bright in sunny weather, for it had tall windows that looked out into gardens at the back of the house, but at the moment the outlook was grey and gloomy and she could barely make out rose beds and a lawn through the streaming glass.

Roy Barton was standing beside a big oak desk to one side of the room and he came across when he saw her, hand outstretched, and smiling. He was quite good-looking, she had forgotten just how good-looking, with thick brown hair that curled slightly over his forehead and brown eyes that regarded her almost anxiously as he came towards her.

'Miss Sutton! I'm so glad you've found us safely; did you have a good journey?'

As he shook hands with her Fern felt herself relax a little. He was just as pleasant as she remembered him, and some of her doubts had already vanished, the rest would no doubt follow them soon. She felt she was going to like Barton's Fen after all. Assigning her to a chair on the other side of the desk, he took a cigarette from a box and lit it before it occurred to him to offer her one.

Shaking her head, Fern smiled. 'No, thank you, I don't.'

'How wise of you!' He smiled ruefully and raised a brow. 'You don't mind if I do?'

It seemed strange for him to be asking if she minded him smoking in his own house, but she supposed if he had difficulty in getting staff, he was prepared to pander to some of the foibles of those he could get. For a second or two, while the smoke from his cigarette drifted before his face, he regarded her from across the desk and Fern felt he was, on the whole, approving. When the smoke cleared and she was able to see his face more clearly, it was clear that he liked what he saw and he leaned forward in his chair.

There was a half-hesitant smile about his mouth that gave him a quite boyish look that was unexpected, and he was shaking his head. 'I hadn't quite realised what a very pretty girl I'd taken on, Miss Sutton. I do hope you won't find it too quiet here for you.' He hastened to add the more practical adjoiner, as if he feared she might take exception to the personal compliment, but Fern saw no fault in it, and she smiled as encouragingly as she knew how.

'Oh, I think I shall like it very well, Mr Barton, although so far what I've seen of the countryside and the weather hasn't been very encouraging.'

She didn't suggest that the landscape looked as if it might be almost as grimly bare even in sunshine, for she could not fairly judge on what she had seen so far, and from what he had told her during her interview, she gathered that he belonged to a local family. It would not do to begin by criticising the environment if it was his native heath.

She assumed he must have the key to her cottage, and she raised the matter as a means of breaking a rather awkward silence. 'You've got the key to my cottage, I expect, haven't you, Mr Barton?'

'Oh yes. Yes, of course, I'd forgotten, you'll be wanting to get in.' He opened a drawer in the desk and
brought out a large old-fashioned iron key, handing
it across the desk to her. 'There you are, Miss Sutton,
I do hope you'll find it comfortable.'

Fern felt a curious thrill as she took it, for it felt
quite different from having the key to her own flat in
town. This was a cottage in the country and close to the
sea, and she suddenly looked forward to seeing her new
possession, no matter how wet and dreary the landscape around it might be. Tucking the key into her
handbag, she smiled across at Roy Barton.

'I'm really looking forward to seeing my cottage in
the country. I have to admit that it was the biggest
single point in deciding me to come.'

The brown eyes warmed as he got up from the desk
and came round to stand beside her. 'Then I'm glad it
was available.' He glanced at his wristwatch and smiled.
'I hope you're not in so much hurry that you can't stay
and have a cup of tea with me before I take you down
to your cottage, Miss Sutton?'

Just as Scott Redman had anticipated, Fern remembered, and she nodded her thanks. 'I'd like that, thank
you.'

He crossed to the door and called to Mrs Dean, then
returned and sat once more behind the desk, one leg
crossed over the other and one booted foot swinging.
It was then that Fern realised he was wearing breeches
and riding boots with the fawn open-necked shirt, and
she thought how much more at home he looked than
he had when he had interviewed her, wearing a lounge
suit and sitting in a hotel room.

'How did you get up here?' he asked. 'Did you manage to get a taxi? Obviously you did, or you'd have been
soaked walking up the track from the bus stop.'

It took Fern a moment or two to decide to tell him what had happened, and when she did, he frowned. Obviously he took the same view she had herself of being made a fool of by Scott Redman, and she had the feeling that he had no better opinion of his other tenant than his housekeeper had. It was not too hard to believe, of course, for the two men were as chalk and cheese; two vastly different characters, yet both attractive men in their own ways.

'It sounds like Redman, to play that kind of a trick on you,' he said. 'I don't much care for the man myself, though he's a good enough tenant and he pays his rent regularly—I can't complain.'

Fern considered the idea of having someone like Scott Redman in permanent residence next door to her, and she found it discomfiting to some extent. 'Is he a fixture in the cottage?' she asked, then laughed and shook her head to deny herself any right to question him about his other tenant. 'I simply wondered if he was likely to be in the other cottage for any length of time, or if he was just holidaying—I've no real business asking, in fact!'

'Oh, but of course you have, if you're to live next door to him,' Roy Barton told her. 'But I'm afraid I don't know just how long he proposes to stay. He told me he was a writer, though I've no idea what he writes or even if he ever does any work at all.' It seemed to occur to him suddenly that he was saying rather a lot to a virtual stranger, and he shook his head in regret. 'Oh well, I've no doubt you'll get along well enough, Miss Sutton. You probably won't see much of him if he's working all day and you're down here.'

'No,' Fern agreed, but wondered if writers worked all the week-end as well. 'No, I don't suppose I shall.'

Fern had scarcely time to close her door before there

was someone rapping on the solid wooden planks, and she had no difficulty in guessing who it would be. She called out for him to come in, for she had not locked the door and it opened with an old-fashioned drop catch.

The first thing she noticed was that the blue shirt had been exchanged for a tan one that added depth to a quite fascinatingly dark sun tan, and he seemed to have rubbed his hair dry without bothering to do much about combing it afterwards. A certain studied carelessness, she felt, was part of Scott Redman's make-up, though she wondered at herself making such a firm assumption after only one brief meeting.

The fact that he was smiling when he walked into the tiny, low-ceilinged room seemed inevitable, and she noticed that he had to duck to avoid hitting his head on the low lintel over the doorway. It was the first time she had met a writer, she thought, and speculated on the kind of things he wrote, without coming to any conclusion.

'Any assistance needed?' he asked, and looked around, as if he expected to see more than her two suitcases standing there at the foot of the stairs.

Fern shook her head. 'I haven't anything to do but unpack a couple of suitcases,' she told him, 'and I can manage that myself, thank you, Mr Redman.'

'Haven't you brought any bits and pieces to make it look more like home?'

It hadn't even occurred to her until now, but Fern supposed it was an idea to add one or two personal touches to the already furnished cottage. She might think about buying one or two things later on, to give the place more warmth and character, but at the moment until she was more sure that she was going to cope with the new and more rigorous environment, it would be as well to leave things as they were.

'I might, later on—I'll see.'

He grinned, and Fern knew it was because he recalled the expression on her face as he drove her
through the dreary wet countryside on the way there.
Those twisty, rain-washed lanes from the station at
Sandmere Halt to Thorpe St Mary had given her a cold
reception and he had studied her face in the driving
mirror when she saw them.

'You do figure on staying here, then? The rain hasn't
scared you off the place?' His grin dared her to admit
how close she had come to turning back, and she glared
at him defiantly.

'No, of course I'm not put off!' Hasty as she was to
deny it, she knew he did not believe her, and she gave
her attention to the small window through which she
could see a patch of clearing sky. 'Nowhere looks its
best in pouring rain,' she told him, 'I can't judge on
what I saw coming here. The rain's stopped now, and
I can take a better view when the sun shines.'

'British fair play, huh?' He was wearing that same
irrepressible grin and it made Fern feel slightly uneasy, for there was a discomfiting boldness in the strong
features that she could not quite slot into a convenient
niche. 'Did you get a cuppa, by the way?' he asked.
'I got everything ready just in case.'

'Yes, I did, thank you.' Making the face she did was
purely involuntary when she recalled the tea she had
been given; she had no intention of belittling Roy
Barton's hospitality.

But he noticed and laughed. 'And you didn't like
it?' he guessed, giving her no time to confirm it. 'That's
a real devil's brew of Frances Dean's, isn't it?'

Fern sought excuses, while mentally forced to agree
with his description of the brew. 'I'm not really very
fond of tea,' she confessed.

Once more that full-throated laughter filled the little

cottage and made it difficult for her not to join in. 'Boy, I never thought I'd see the day when a Limey admitted to not liking tea!'

'I'm not completely averse to it.' She wanted to put matters right, and not let him think she had not appreciated it at all. 'It's just that I prefer coffee on the whole.'

'Then come next door and let me make you some coffee!'

He seemed determined to do something to help, and it was difficult to go on refusing, particularly since she felt rather as if she owed him something for having mistaken him for a taxi driver. 'That's very good of you, Mr Redman, but there's really no need to put you to the trouble. I have everything here that I need.'

'No trouble at all,' he assured her.

'But——'

'Oh, come on, honey! Come down off that high horse for a couple of minutes, will you?'

Fern's chin angled warningly, but she didn't see how she could go on refusing. She was not, however, prepared to allow any suggestion that she was being snobbish. 'I'm not on a high horse, as you call it, Mr Redman, but since you've been so kind——'

'Good!' He cut her short, which Fern suspected was typical of him. 'I'll just sling your bags upstairs, then we'll go round to my place for coffee.'

From the sounds that followed, Fern thought he probably had literally slung her suitcase upstairs, for he was down again in a couple of minutes, taking her arm in uninhibited friendliness as he led her along to the cottage next door. Passing from one to the other, she smelled the fresh clean air and breathed deeply and appreciatively. The rain was finished and the wind had dropped a little; it smelled good.

Scott Redman's coffee smelled good too, and it tasted

even better, and he refused to let her help wash up
their cups when it was finished, but left her in one of
the huge armchairs the cottage was furnished with
while he took them out to the kitchen and washed
them himself while she relaxed for a few minutes.

She hadn't realised quite how tired she was, and she
half closed her eyes as she gazed across at the tiny window, her mind in a daze and wandering over all that
had happened since she left her flat for the last time
that morning. She was so preoccupied that for a
moment she did not register the fact that there was
someone peering in through the window at her, and
the shock of suddenly realising it made her cry out in
surprise.

She jerked herself upright in the big chair, but the
face had already disappeared, so that by the time Scott
Redman came hurrying in from the kitchen she was
already wondering if she really had seen someone or
if she had merely imagined it because she was so tired.
His hands still dripping water, Scott Redman bent over
her until his rugged dark face was only inches from
her own as he stared down at her.

'What in hell's the matter?' he demanded.

'I—I saw someone at the window.' She flicked an
anxious tongue over her lips and felt incredibly silly
suddenly when she saw the look of utter disbelief on
his face.

Straightening up, he stood with his hands back-
turned on his hips, looking down at her with a shadow
of a grin hovering about his mouth. 'Surely the fens
haven't got to you already, honey! Or maybe you just
dropped off for a minute, huh? I thought you looked
kind of droopy when I left you—you've had a heavy
day.'

Fern struggled upright in the massive chair and the
look she gave him was as much reproachful as indig-

nant. 'I'm not in the least droopy, Mr Redman, and neither am I in the habit of seeing things. I definitely saw a face at the window.'

'What kind of a face, for Pete's sake?' He so obviously found the whole thing amusing that Fern felt like hitting him. 'Was it the Phantom of the Fens? You're just seeing things, honey, because you're tired.'

'I am *not* seeing things! I tell you I saw a face—a small face with a lot of blond hair.'

It was when he started to laugh that she got to her feet, determined not to be the butt of his humour again. But he was shaking his head and one hand persuaded her down into the chair again; with those strong fingers on her shoulder, there was little option for her and she subsided, though with bad grace. Scott Redman sat down facing her, his hands clasped together between his knees and his elbows on his knees as he leaned towards her.

'I guess you saw young Jem,' he told her, and smiled as he went on to explain. 'He's the housekeeper's boy; a funny kid but not crazy or anything like that. He's just lonely, I guess.'

It seemed so simple an explanation that Fern felt more foolish than ever for having made so much fuss. It was hard to face the fact that twice within a couple of hours she had made a fool of herself in this man's eyes, and she wished there was some easy way for her to simply get up and walk back to her own cottage without further loss of dignity. An upward glance revealed the fact that he was still faintly smiling, and it was all she could do to remain cool and polite.

'You seem to have a very poor opinion of me,' she suggested, and sensed the mockery in the eyes that watched her so intently. 'You obviously think I'm a complete idiot.'

'Oh no, not a complete one, honey!' She looked up

swiftly when he laughed and it was as if he suddenly
became very serious for a second while she looked at
him. His eyes traversed her face, feature by feature
until they lighted on her mouth, then he smiled slowly.
'You're going to have your work cut out keeping the
lord of the manor at bay,' he said, and she frowned at
him curiously. 'Roy Barton, the squire of Barton's
Fen! I hope you're strong-willed, honey; that boyish
charm can be pretty devastating, so I've heard!'

She was blushing again, Fern realised with horror,
and got to her feet, her eyes bright and angry. Neighbour or not, Scott Redman was obviously the kind of
man who, given an inch, would take a mile, and she
had no intention of allowing that. Looking at him
down the length of her nose, she angled her chin.

'I think you've said enough, Mr Redman, and I
think it's time I went. I've a lot to do, and——'

'And you figure I'm being too sassy, is that it?' He
was laughing at her still, Fern realised angrily. 'Well,
I'm sorry you feel that way, duchess, but I'm just not
used to your ways yet—give me time and I'll learn.'

'I doubt it!' Chin high, she walked to the door and
opened it, speaking to him over her shoulder without
actually turning round. 'Thank you for the coffee, Mr
Redman—goodbye!'

The deep-sounding chuckle that followed her to the
door made her roll her hands tightly as she went outside into the cool fresh air, and his voice mocked her
as she pulled the door to behind her. 'So long, duchess!'

CHAPTER TWO

It was while she was tidying the kitchen before she left for work the following morning that Fern became aware of a masculine voice raised in song coming from the cottage next door. The walls were very thin and from the sounds that accompanied the singing, Scott Redman was evidently having his morning bath. She glanced at her wristwatch and shrugged—no doubt writers could choose their own hours of work, but she would have thought that eight-fifty was rather late to be just getting up if one worked seriously for a living.

Everything as yet was strange to her, and while she tidied up the kitchen Fern thought more about bringing in some things of her own choice that would give the place a more personal air. Although perhaps it might be as well to wait until the trial period was over and she was more certain that she had made the right decision before she did anything definite about it. It was nevertheless an idea to be considered, and it surprised her momentarily to remember that it had originally been Scott Redman's suggestion.

The quite good baritone next door was rendering a tune she was unfamiliar with but which was quite pleasant to listen to, and she thought the words sounded French. It was difficult to tell for certain through the dividing wall, but it certainly wasn't English and, since she had decided that her neighbour was Canadian, it was quite possible to believe that he was a French-Canadian.

A mirror was hung conveniently on the wall near the

front door, and Fern took advantage of it to take a last
look at herself before she left the house. Her feet had
scarcely touched the single flagstone that did service as
a front step when the door right next to hers opened
suddenly and the rugged, tanned face of her neighbour
looked round at her.

'Hi! Settling in O.K.?'

Fern closed her door firmly and put the heavy iron
key into her handbag as she answered him. She hated
feeling so gauche, and wished she had not made such
a fool of herself yesterday; somehow it seemed to give
him such an advantage over her and she did not like
the idea of that at all.

'Good morning, Mr Redman; everything's fine, thank
you.'

'Good!' Intensely blue eyes regarded her for a
second as she turned and started towards the communal
front gate. It was set between the two patches of garden
and was no more than four or five strides long, but it
felt like a mile to Fern with Scott Redman watching
and, she suspected, laughing at her. 'Say, do you ride?'

It was the complete unexpectedness of the question
that made her turn and stare at him, for she could not
imagine why he should see fit to raise the question of
whether or not she rode at this hour of the day when
he knew she was on her way to work. But he had suc-
ceeded in holding her attention and she stood with a
hand on the gate looking back at him and shaking her
head.

He wasn't fully dressed, for it was only a matter of
minutes since she had heard him singing in the bath,
and she could see the top half of a naked brown torso
above the blue slacks, and there was a towel slung
carelessly around his neck. He stood with one arm
leaned on the door jamb, and he was looking at her

enquiringly, so that she hastily snatched herself back
to his question.

'Ride? No, I don't.' She frowned curiously. 'Why?'

The grin was seemingly inevitable and it split his
dark face to show teeth that looked incredibly white
and strong. 'You will, honey, you will! Your boss will
have you on a horse before you've been here five
minutes, I promise you!'

'I doubt that very much, Mr Redman; I've never
been on a horse in my life!'

Not at all sure where the conversation could be leading, and conscious of the passing time, Fern was nevertheless curious enough to linger for a moment or two
longer. He must have had some reason for making the
statement he had and, with an eye to possible future
awkwardness with her employer, she tried to discover
what it was.

'I can't imagine why Mr Barton would be likely to
think an ability to ride a horse an essential part of
being a good secretary,' she said, and he shook his head.

'It has nothing to do with being a good secretary.'

'Then what——'

'Oh, honey!' The blue eyes mocked her and she knew
he was laughing at her, even though it was less obvious
than it had been at other times. 'The lord of the manor
never considers anyone complete unless they can ride
a horse, and he's going to want you to be a paragon of
all virtues.' He swept a long slow gaze over her trim
figure and slender legs and smiled. 'You've got a hell
of a good start, but he won't see you as the perfect
woman unless you learn to ride.'

The implication was unmistakable and Fern put on
her most chilling manner, the gold flecks dancing in her
eyes as she looked at him, and a hint of a flush in her
cheeks. 'Since you're so scathing about it, I gather you
don't ride either!'

He eased himself lazily away from the door frame and came out to lean on the wall beside the door, slippered feet crossed one over the other and his arms folded on a broad chest. His hair, she noticed, was still damp and looked slightly less blond than it had yesterday, but the grin was as much in evidence as ever.

'Oh, sure I do,' he told her. 'Only I don't ride with the local hunt, the way his lordship does.' The blue eyes twinkled at her wickedly. 'I guess I'm not gentleman enough to fit in.'

'Do you want to?'

'Not particularly!'

It was ridiculous standing there talking to him when she should be on her way, Fern thought, but somehow the temptation to linger was irresistible. There was a hint of malice in the gleam of his eyes, she noted uneasily, and she could well imagine that he would not fit easily into the local scene. Certainly not as well as her employer.

It was easy to imagine Roy Barton following the hunt, as to the manner born, but the thought of Scott Redman in hunting pink and following the traditional sport of the country squires just wasn't credible; he would appear much more at home on a cattle ranch. And he didn't even look remotely like her conception of a writer.

Recalling herself suddenly, she glanced hastily at her wristwatch and shook her head. 'I really have to go, Mr Redman. I'm supposed to be in the office at nine, and I'm going to be late.'

'Like me to run you down in the car? It's sure to be kind of sticky along the trail after all that rain.'

'Oh no; no, thank you!' She was very sure about it, and she saw another grin spread across his face at her refusal; a vaguely rueful one this time.

'O.K., duchess, have it your way!' He took the towel

from around his neck and rubbed it over his hair. 'I guess I'm not fit to be seen with a lady, only half-dressed like this—what would your boss say?' A careless wave of his hand dismissed her attempt to retort, and he turned back into the cottage. 'So long, duchess—see you!'

She objected to the name he called her, but this was not the time to stop and make her protest, for she was already bound to be late. She tried to hurry as she made her way along the rutted track, and called herself all kinds of a fool to have stopped and talked for so long with a man she did not even like. Being late on her very first morning was not the impression she had hoped to make, and she hoped Roy Barton wouldn't take it as an indication of future occasions.

To make matters worse, yesterday's rain had turned the ground into a quagmire, and it was only by skirting the track itself and walking on the bordering strip of grass that she could get by without becoming bogged down in mud. If this was a sample of the conditions she could expect, it might be as well to get a small motor-scooter for getting to and from work. A car was out of the question, she simply couldn't afford it, but a scooter would at least ensure that she got to work without getting her feet muddy.

The front door was ajar when she arrived and she hesitated only a moment before pushing it wider, tapping lightly with her knuckles as she stepped inside. She had barely set foot in the hall when Mrs Dean, the housekeeper, came out from a door at the far end of the hall and came across to meet her. From the look on her face Fern gathered that she considered it a liberty to simply walk in, although almost certainly the door had been left open for that purpose.

'Good morning.'

No name, Fern noticed, just a swift and very critical

scrutiny of her clothes with narrowed brown eyes. She looked no more friendly this morning than she had yesterday and Fern felt a certain jolt of impatience. There seemed to be more setbacks than encouragement so far at Barton's Fen, and she counted her cottage neighbour among them—Mrs Dean was another.

Determinedly friendly, even in the face of discouragement, Fern gave her a smile as she made her way towards the office she had been shown into yesterday. 'Good morning, Mrs Dean, I'm afraid I'm a little late. Is Mr Barton waiting for me?'

'Mr Barton's still out for his morning ride,' the housekeeper informed her, not without some malicious satisfaction, Fern guessed. 'You're supposed to go right in and find the jobs he's left you to do.'

'He asked you to tell me that?'

'No, but it's what he did with the last one!' The light brown eyes speculated on her response, but Fern was not about to be roused into quarrelling with the housekeeper on her first day.

'Then that's what I'll do—thank you, Mrs Dean.'

Her training as a secretary came to her aid, or she felt sure she would have been rude to the woman. It was a pity she had been late on her first morning, though, for she felt certain that Mrs Dean would tell Roy Barton about it. Without another word the housekeeper turned and went back to her own quarters, but Fern still had certain misgivings. It was just possible that the staff shortage at Barton's Fen owed something to Mrs Dean as well as the bleakness of the environment.

The office looked very much different this morning with the sun shining, and it did something to raise her spirits a little. The gardens outside looked very much more inviting than the flat landscape beyond them and much better than they had yesterday in the pouring rain. A gravel path passed under the windows and wound its way round out of sight again behind a rose pergola, and round beds of roses blossomed against a background of lush green lawn, fresh after yesterday's rain.

It seemed a little stuffy in the room, so Fern opened a window, then set about discovering what work had been left for her. The bigger desk at the other side of the room she knew was the one Roy Barton used, but a smaller one with a typewriter standing ready on it had a pleasanter view of the garden, and that served as another prospect to cheer her.

The machine she had been provided with was fairly old but still in good working order, and there was an adequate supply of everything she was likely to need. A number of letters written in longhand lay beside the typewriter and they, she assumed, were the work that had been left for her to do.

She had just inserted the first sheets of paper and carbon into the machine when she heard the front door open and lowered voices in the hall. One of them she recognised as the housekeeper's, and she had no difficulty believing that Roy Barton was being informed of her late arrival. Pulling a wry face, she waited for the door to open, and when it did she was struck once more by the fact of what a good-looking man he was.

The smile she gave him was purely instinctive and took no account of the fact that his housekeeper had probably just been regaling him with her shortcomings. Rather it took advantage of the fact that he was so obviously pleased to see her.

'Good morning, Mr Barton.'

'Good morning, Miss Sutton!' He came across to her and stood just the other side of her desk, looking down at her in such a way that it was obvious he liked what he saw. 'Have you settled yourself in all right?'

'Very well, thank you.' She looked up and pulled a rueful face. 'But I'm afraid I shall have to start out a bit earlier in the morning from now on than I did today. I was late this morning, and that isn't one of my failings as a rule.'

'Oh, good heavens, that doesn't matter!' From his expression she knew she had been right about Mrs Dean's mischiefmaking, but he was shaking his head to dismiss any suggestion of taking it seriously. 'You have to get used to things first and that track is longer than you'd think when you have to walk it. It's horribly muddy this morning too; Caleb was mud up to his belly!'

'Caleb?'

She had a very good idea who Caleb was, but considered it politic to let him tell her himself. 'Oh, Caleb's my horse, or one of them—I ride every morning, rain or shine.' It was inevitable, Fern knew, just as Scott Redman had forecast. Roy Barton's brown eyes settled on her earnestly across the desk. 'Do you ride, Miss Sutton?'

Wondering just how far short she would fall in his estimation if she admitted not knowing one end of a rein from the other, Fern shook her head. 'No, I don't.'

'Oh, that's a pity!'

He ran a hand through his hair, and hesitated for a moment so that Fern took the initiative, trying to settle the matter one way or the other. 'Is it essential, Mr Barton? I mean, nothing was said, and it isn't usual for a secretary to have to know how to ride——'

'No, no, of course it isn't essential!' He smiled and she was struck by the thought of how nice he was. Nice was exactly the word; one couldn't use anything more dramatic or forceful, as with Scott Redman. Roy Barton was essentially nice, and she liked him. 'It's just that I'm rather a fanatic about horses,' he confessed, 'and

I rather hoped you'd be able to join me on a ride sometimes.'

'That would have been nice, but I'm afraid I've never been on a horse in my life.'

'Have you something against horses?'

Fern shook her head. 'Nothing at all, except that they're so big and I'm a bit nervous of getting too close in case they use those big teeth!' She laughed as if it was a joke, but in fact it was near truth.

'Oh, no; Caleb certainly wouldn't! Perhaps I could teach you.' The offer was rather unexpected and for a moment Fern hesitated, and in doing so possibly gave him the wrong impression. He took in her slender figure in a swift appraisal, and smiled. 'You look as if you'd take to it, and you'd certainly look well on a horse.'

It was startling to find him so ready to press the matter and she shook her head more firmly. 'I don't think so, Mr Barton, I really don't care for the idea of riding horses, though it's very kind of you to offer to teach me.'

'It would be as much, or more, for my pleasure as yours—and it would sound much more friendly if you called me Roy.' He leaned slightly forward with his hands resting on her desk and Fern tried hard to control a sudden fluttering sensation in her pulse as she smiled up at him.

'Then you'd better call me Fern,' she told him lightly. 'It's a silly kind of name, I know, but it's the only one I have, and at least it can't be shortened.'

'It shouldn't *be* shortened!' His sober response was in direct contrast to her own lighthearted manner, and he held her eyes for a moment with a boldness that she would have thought more characteristic of Scott Redman. 'It's a lovely name, Fern, and it suits you perfectly.'

'Thank you. Actually I was named after a plant because my mother was a naturalist before she was married. She taught botany and went back to it afterwards, until she died, in fact.' She smiled and glanced up through her lashes at him. 'I suppose I'm lucky I wasn't called something Latin and unpronounceable!'

'Fern is lovely—it reminds me of cool streams and woods, and I shall certainly use it.'

'I hope you will.' She felt strangely elated, but when she glanced down at her desk the pile of letters by her typewriter reminded her that she had not yet done a stroke of work, and she pulled a face. 'I'm not making a very good first impression, I'm afraid. First I come late, and then spend all my time talking instead of getting on with these letters you left for me. If I don't make a start you'll begin to wish you'd never set eyes on me!'

A hand reached out and stayed hers when it was half-way to the pile of letters, squeezing gently. 'I doubt that very much,' he said.

It was a relief to have things working out better than she had first expected, and after three days at Barton's Fen, Fern was beginning to think she had made a good move after all. The work itself was not very demanding, although there were any number of forms to be filled out, connected with Ministry returns, and she got along very well with Roy Barton. Perhaps things could have been a little better if Mrs Dean had been as ready to be friendly, but she saw very little of the house-keeper, so it was not too difficult to ignore her incivility.

She had so far learned that her employer managed rather than owned Barton's Fen, although he was the owner's cousin. Who the absent owner was no one had so far enlightened her, but it was of no real concern and made no difference at all to her own position, so that she was no more than mildly curious.

The persistent wind off the sea, she was beginning to realise, was something she would have to learn to live with, for it seldom let up, rain or fine, and when it rained it made sure that everything got thoroughly soaked. So far the balance had been more in favour of the sun, but when Fern woke to find it raining heavily once more, she sighed resignedly as she got out of bed.

No matter what the weather it seemed her day was bound to start with a song from the bathroom next door, and on a wet morning like today Fern was almost grateful for its cheerfully abandoned volume, even if it did give the illusion that the man who raised his voice so happily was actually in the same cottage with her. The thin dividing walls had once or twice given her a disturbing sense of intimacy with her neighbour.

The track to the house was going to be almost impassable on foot and she thought once more about getting a motor scooter; as it was she would need a raincoat and wellingtons to make the journey. With her hair tucked up under a hat that matched her raincoat and the collar turned up around her face, Fern took her customary look in the mirror beside the door before leaving. Her hand was already on the latch when a loud thumping on the other side of the wall made her snatch it back as if she had been stung, and she caught her breath sharply.

'Hold it while I get the car round!' Scott Redman's voice reached her with startling clarity through the wall, and she was too surprised to argue for a moment, although obviously an argument was anticipated. 'And don't think of turning down a lift in this weather, duchess!' the voice went on. 'Even you're not that proud!'

'There's no——'

She was cut short by a loud slap, as if he had hit the wall with the flat of his hand, and she heard him laugh. 'Hold everything, duchess, I'm on my way!'

It was useless to try and argue in the circumstances, and the sound of a door banging suggested that it was too late anyway; he had gone out through the back door to fetch his car. She was bound to get soaked even taking half a dozen steps in such a downpour, along that muddy track, and yet she still had the irresistible urge to refuse his offer and make her own way. It didn't make sense, and she admitted it, but it did not prevent her from feeling strangely uneasy about accepting his help.

The rain was coming from the rear of the house so she stood with the front door open, listening for the sound of a car being started, and only seconds later it came into her line of vision. It stopped with the passenger door directly opposite the garden gate, and Scott leaned across to open it while she ran down the path. She fumbled for a moment with the catch on the gate and got quite wet even in those few seconds.

'Pardon me for not being a gentleman,' he said as she slid on to the seat beside him, 'but there's no sense in me standing out in the rain to hold the door for you.'

'None at all,' Fern agreed, 'I didn't expect you to.'

He smelled of some pleasantly woody after-shave, and she suspected he had not long come from his bath, for there was a warm, damp look about him. He had on a white tee-shirt and navy slacks, and his hair was slick and wet, except where it was beginning to dry just above his ears; there it was blond and slightly curled. His arms were bare, strong and tanned, like his face, and she felt a curious little shiver of sensation slip along her spine when she noticed them and the long hands on the steering wheel.

He turned his head suddenly and caught her eye, his left eyelid swiftly lowered in a broad wink. 'Good morning!'

Fern could do nothing about the responsive smile that briefly touched her lips, and she inclined her head. 'Good morning, Mr Redman.'

She found his closeness disconcerting and in some curious way resented it. It wasn't as if he was very good-looking like Roy Barton, or as if he made constant references to how attractive he found her, as Roy did. It was just something about the man himself that made her feel curiously uneasy, and she suspected it had something to do with the fact that he had had all too many opportunities to laugh at her since she arrived.

'It's very good of you to go to this trouble,' she added.

He was leaned forward in his seat trying to peer through the streaming windscreen and cursing the mud that splashed up as they jolted along the rutted track, but just briefly he half-turned his head and grinned at her, disconcertingly honest. 'It's no trouble, honey, I have my rent to pay so I figured I may as well bring it up myself as let the lord of the manor collect it himself. Seeing as you stood a good chance of being bogged down in this lot, I figured I may as well do two for the price of one and bring you in style.'

'Well, it was very good of you, but you shouldn't have turned out simply on my account. I didn't expect it of you.'

Once more that bright blue gaze mocked her, while one hand reached out to rub at the windscreen and try and clear it. 'You figure I'd let you walk up here in this? That's not very flattering, duchess. Just because I'm a wild colonial it doesn't mean I don't know how to treat a lady.'

Whether or not his indignation was genuine, Fern

could not have said, but she felt a niggling suspicion
that he was baiting her, and she pushed a strand of
dark hair up under her hat while she spoke. 'I didn't
suggest otherwise, Mr Redman, though I had guessed
you were a Canadian, which is what I presume you
mean by being a colonial.'

She was asking him to confirm it and he did so with
another grin. 'Clever girl,' he congratulated her. 'Most
folks can't tell which side we come from—Yanks or
Canadians, it's all one to them!'

'You're a long way from home, whichever it is,' Fern
told him, watching the flat wet fields go by on either
side. 'What made you come to Lincolnshire?'

'What made you?' The blue eyes were brightly challenging, and she shook her head.

'I saw an advert for this job and I felt like a change.'

'And I was looking for somewhere quiet to work.'
He too looked out at the streaming countryside, and
pulled a face. 'And God knows there's nowhere quieter
than Thorpe St Mary, it's the back of beyond!'

Fern was still unwilling to condemn her new environment too soon, and she accepted that he was probably
right, but qualified it a little. 'It's very peaceful,' she
said. 'It should suit a writer. What do you write, Mr
Redman?'

The broad shoulders heaved carelessly and he did not
turn and look at her this time when he answered. 'Oh,
this and that.'

He was obviously not going to give much away, and
Fern understood why Roy had been so dubious about
his actual purpose the first time he spoke of him. Still,
if he wanted to keep his secrets to himself, it was up to
him, she looked out of the window once more at the
rain.

'Well, it's quiet enough to suit anyone here,' she said.

The long hands on the wheel wrenched suddenly to

one side when a particularly slippery patch of mud
threatened to send them off course, and Scott was
cursing as he fought to keep on the muddy track.
Through the windscreen Fern caught sight of another
car coming round the bend from the drive and more
curses condemned the need to take evasive action while
it passed.

There was something familiar about the driver in
the brief glimpse Fern had of him, and she turned in
her seat to try and look back, her vision blurred by the
rain. 'Wasn't that Roy—Mr Barton?'

'Yeah, pity he missed you, isn't it?'

Fern looked at him and blinked, uncertain just how
serious he was, then clung on grimly as he turned into
the curving drive in front of the house and braked.
'You don't think he's going to my cottage, do you?'

He was out of his seat and holding the door for her
while he answered, standing back under the edge of the
porch, so as not to get too wet. 'I'd say it was quite
likely,' he told her, and his apparent amusement at the
idea angered Fern.

'Well, if he is I don't find it funny!' she snapped,
pulling off her hat and letting her hair fall about her
face the way it most always did. 'If you recognised him
and knew he was going down to fetch me why didn't
you signal to him?'

'You think he'd have taken any notice?' he asked,
and grinned at her in a way that suggested he was quite
aware of Roy's opinion of him. 'Of course if he saw you
as he went past us, he might be already on his way
back.'

Fern stood at the opening of the porch watching the
entrance to the drive. 'I hope he saw us,' she said.

The bright blue eyes that watched her in turn had
a slightly impatient gleam that she did not see for a
moment, and they suggested both mockery and exasper-

ation. 'He saw *us*, honey, he couldn't miss the car, but he'll only come back if he realised it was you I had with me. Anyway,' he pointed out, 'he's not going to get wet, is he? Don't make a major crisis out of it, duchess.'

'I wish you wouldn't call me that stupid name!' Fern's voice was sharp, sharper perhaps than she intended, and one light brow remarked on the fact.

'What should I call you?' he asked. 'Fern, or maybe Fernie?'

She was disgruntled enough to forget that he had just done her a service by bringing her there and preventing her from getting soaked, and she stuck out her chin, the gold flecks in her eyes sparkling bright. 'You could try Miss Sutton,' she suggested, her voice unsteady.

'Oh, the unfriendly type, eh?' It obviously took a lot to deter him, for he was still smiling; an impudent, rakish sort of smile, and he bowed his head mockingly. 'O.K., duchess, you stay up there among the cool and beautiful goddesses, if that's where you see yourself belonging; maybe the lord of the manor likes that type. Me, I go for flesh and blood women myself!' He turned and pushed open the door that was already ajar as it always was in the mornings, then he turned and grinned at her as irrepressibly as ever while he waited for her to join him. 'Are you coming in, or are you going to wait there for your lord and master to return?'

There was no time for Fern to decide one way or the other, for she could hear a car coming and a moment later it came splashing through the mud into the drive. Scott Redman strolled back and stood beside her while it pulled up immediately behind his own car and Roy got out, running in under the shelter of the porch before he said anything. He glanced from one to the other with such evident suspicion that it was

clear what was going on in his mind—a fact that seemed
to amuse at least one of his callers.

'Good morning.' He once more flicked his glance
between them. 'I don't often get two callers this early
in the day.'

'It's the end of the week,' Scott reminded him, and
glanced with wicked meaning at Fern. 'I figured I'd
mix a little business with pleasure—pay my rent and
bring Fern to work at the same time.'

His casual use of her first name made Roy frown,
and Fern wondered if that wasn't just the effect it was
meant to achieve. 'I had the same idea,' he told him,
leading the way inside. 'Only it seems I was too late.'

'If I'd known——' Fern began, then caught Scott
Redman's eye on her and did not go on.

'You weren't to know, how could you?' Roy told her,
but from his expression it was clear that he did not like
being forestalled and it crossed Fern's mind to wonder
if she could expect him at her cottage door very early
the next time it rained. 'The next time it's raining so
hard, Fern, just wait for me and I'll come down for you.
There'll be no need to bother anyone else.'

'Oh, it was no bother at all,' Scott assured him
blithely. 'And it might console you to know that Fern
would much rather not have come with me, only even
she couldn't face walking up here in this downpour,
so she made the best of a bad job.'

'Oh, but I didn't——'

'I'm wrong?' Scott looked almost naïvely pleased at
the idea and Fern wished it was possible to make him
drop the subject. 'I'm glad to hear that, honey, I
thought you hated the idea of me driving you.'

His manner seemed to put Roy at a loss for a moment
or two, but he quickly recovered and glanced at Fern
as she walked across the hall with him, then looked

back at Scott over his shoulder. 'I'll see about your rent first,' he told him. 'Will you come into the office?'

Fern was already sitting down at her desk and sorting through the day's work when Roy handed back the rent book, and she looked up instinctively when she felt she was being watched. Vivid blue eyes held hers steadily for a moment and Scott Redman grinned, then he turned and a careless hand gave her a half-salute as he strolled across to the door, one eyelid fluttering briefly in a wink as he turned to close the door.

'See you, duchess!'

Roy frowned at the closed door for several seconds before he sat down behind his desk, and his hands moved with an angry jerkiness among the papers on it. His stormy reaction surprised Fern for a moment, for he seemed to take it all so much to heart.

'Uncouth devil!' He glanced across at her, as if he sought her reaction, then shook his head. 'Shall we get on?'

CHAPTER THREE

NEITHER of the two Fen Cottages had a very big garden, but a patch of green and a couple of hardy rose bushes flourished in the heavy clay on Fern's side of the dividing path, and some bright orange marigolds blazed defiantly along Scott Redman's narrow border. A tall and straggly box hedge completely enclosed both properties except where the front gate broke its continuity, and a gap at the back of Number One allowed her neighbour access to the tumbledown shed that he used to garage his car.

It was quite surprising, therefore, for Fern to spot an intruder from her window. She had just finished her lunch when she spotted a small boy with his hands in the pockets of his shorts, wandering around the grass path that surrounded her rose bushes, looking as if he was not sure what to do next. He was small, no more than six years old, she guessed, and blond with huge blue eyes that looked at her in a vaguely sheepish way when she appeared at the window.

She had been on the point of leaving when she saw him, and she saw no point in doing anything about him until she had let herself out and put the key into her bag. He looked curiously familiar, and yet she was quite sure she hadn't seen him before, and she turned and smiled at him because she had a genuine liking for children.

'Hello, where did you spring from?'

The snub toe of a shoe kicked at the grass bordering

45

the path and he studiously avoided looking at her.
'Nowhere.'

It was a typically childish answer, and Fern smiled
to herself as he came and joined her on the path, his
head bowed and obviously not quite sure what he ought
to say or do next. 'I see.' She smiled at the bowed head
and put a hand on his shoulder as she started towards
the gate. 'Well, where do you live? Close by?'

The village of Thorpe St Mary was only a short walk
away, so he could quite easily have come from there,
but what she could not see was why he should be hang-
ing around in her front garden at a time of day when
he should surely have been at school. She was about to
raise the question with her unexpected visitor when
the door of the other cottage opened and the boy beside
her turned swiftly.

'Hi, Jem, how are you?'

The boy's face was beaming, and he glanced up at
Fern as if he did not understand her frown. Obviously
he knew Scott Redman, and if that was the case she
could leave him to deal with the matter while she went
back to work.

'I'm better now, thank you.' The boy's voice was
small and piping and when she half-turned as she
opened the gate she noticed how tiny he looked beside
the man's towering leanness.

He was looking at her curiously too, she noticed, and
Scott Redman grinned as he ushered the boy along the
path towards her. 'Have you met Miss Sutton yet?'

The child was shaking his head and Fern's frown reappeared for a second when she realised that by invol-
ving her so directly Scott had virtually made certain
that she was going to be late back. The two of them
came and joined her where she stood beside the gate,
and the boy was still eyeing her curiously, wondering
just who she was. The mocking gleam in his compan-

ion's eyes was now almost to be expected, and he stood
with one hand on a wooden pale and the other on the
boy's head.

'Jem, this is Miss Sutton.'

He added no surname, she noticed, but simply called
him Jem, and she was instantly reminded of her very
first evening there, nearly a week ago, when she had
sat in an armchair in Scott Redman's cottage and cried
out at the sight of a face at the window. The name Jem
had been mentioned then, as an alternative to the face
being simply a figment of her imagination. Looking
at the boy now, she could believe that it was him she
had seen, with his shock of blond hair and huge eyes.

'You remember Jem?' She caught the bright glitter
of laughter and hastily looked away. 'Miss Sutton works
for Mr Barton as his secretary, Jem—you know what
that is?' The boy shook his head. 'It means that she
types letters and fills in forms—among other things.'

He meant her to read something into that, even if
the boy didn't, but she chose to ignore it and turned to
the boy instead. 'I remember catching sight of you once
before,' she told Jem. 'The first day I came here.'

'The Phantom of the Fens!' Scott reminded her with
a laugh. 'I told you it could have been Jem, didn't I?'

'Yes, you did, Mr Redman, and of course you were
right! I imagine you have a habit of being right when
you have prior knowledge!' Yet again she experienced
that discomfiting sense of inadequacy, and she did not
enjoy the sensation at all. Glancing once more at her
wristwatch, she opened the gate and stood in the opening, ready to leave. 'And I really must go, or I shall be
late back.'

'Hey, Jem, why don't you walk back to the house
with Miss Sutton?' Fern had no time to object that she
had little enough time to make her own way back,
without having to slow her pace to that of a six-year-

old, before Scott Redman was coming up with another
idea. 'Or better still, why don't I run both of you back
in the car? I guess it's kind of muddy on the trail, huh,
Jem?'

The child, of course, was almost bound to agree, but
to Fern the prospect of once more arriving for work in
his car was less agreeable, and she was already shaking
her head almost before the suggestion had been voiced.
'There's really no need to, Mr Redman, I can quite
easily walk—I've already done the trip twice today.'

Scott looked as if he saw her protest as inevitable, as
she supposed it was, though he did nothing beyond
briefly arch a brow before he turned away. He was not
a man who easily took no for an answer, she guessed,
and he was striding swiftly back towards the cottage
with the boy in pursuit, taking the side path that led
to the makeshift garage at the back.

Fern saw no reason why she need wait there while
they fetched the car, and it took only a second or two
for her to make up her mind. She could still walk, as she
had planned to do, and if he still insisted on giving her
a lift the rest of the way when they caught up with her
then at least she would not have to do the whole journey with him.

The air was fresh and not as warm as it had been
when she made the same journey home to lunch, and
she wondered if they were going to get more rain. If so
she was likely to be making the return journey in Roy
Barton's car, for she knew without doubt that he would
bring her home. Roy had not been at all happy about
her driving up there with Scott Redman, and it sometimes troubled her vaguely that he was quite so obviously annoyed that anyone else should pay her any
attention.

The track was very muddy and once or twice she
had to tread very carefully, but she was beginning to

take such things in her stride, and she had worn boots
as a matter of course, as well as keeping to the firmer
footing of the grass verge alongside the rutted track.
But as she once more sought more firm ground she
pondered on her perversity where Scott Redman was
concerned.

He had offered to drive her, a perfectly reasonable
thing to do, and yet she had refused. She had even set
out on foot rather than wait for him to fetch his car;
it had been instinctive to refuse, as it always was whenever he offered her help, and it really did not make
sense when she thought about it. It was simply that——

A loud blast on a car horn startled her so much that
she slipped and almost fell to her knees in the mud,
then the car drew up beside her, its tyres gouging deeply
into the muddy tracks when he braked. Leaning across
from the front seat, Scott opened the rear door for her,
and she noticed that Jem was already installed in the
front with him. While she hesitated, Scott sat with his
arm along the back of his seat, mocking her hesitation,
and Jem watched, curious and not altogether sure of
of her, she guessed.

'Come on, duchess, take the back seat, you'll feel
more at home there, won't you?'

There was nothing for it, and she climbed meekly
into the back, reminded as she did so of her first ever
journey to Barton's Fen, when she had mistaken his
car for a taxi. It was an occasion she preferred to forget,
though it wasn't easy with those vivid blue eyes there
to remind her.

'Thank you.' She subsided into the luxury of soft
leather and wondered how she could ever have
imagined it was a taxi. 'It's very muddy or I wouldn't
bother you.'

'No bother, honey!'

When the car restarted she was free for a moment of

that disconcerting gaze, but only for a moment, and then she caught him watching her via the driving mirror, as he had on that first occasion, and she clenched her hands tightly on her lap. It was incredible that any man could make her feel so uneasy and so inadequate, when she had always prided herself on being self-possessed, and she resented it bitterly without having the least idea what she could do about it.

When she was sure that he was completely occupied with driving the car, Fern gave her attention to studying him from the back with a kind of curious resentment. His thick hair curled slightly just above his ears and above the broad brow, and its fairness contrasted strongly with a tanned neck and throat. In profile it was a hawkish face but for thick light brown lashes that gentled the strong lines of it, and the wide humorous mouth that was very slightly lopsided when he smiled or laughed.

A blue shirt stretched across broad shoulders and the dark shadow of tanned skin showed through whenever he leaned forward or moved his arms. He was not a man she could think of as ordinary, and yet it was not his physical appearance that made him stand apart, but some indefinable something that she found impossible to specify as yet.

'There you go!' He had stopped short of the gates, she realised when she brought herself hastily back to earth, and he leaned across to open her door before she could do it for herself. The inevitable grin creased his face with a myriad lines in the tanned skin, and he nodded towards the boy as he got out on to the track. 'Deliver young Jem, will you, honey? He's been laid up with a cold and he probably sneaked out without being seen.'

'Yes, of course.' She slammed the door closed automatically, then put a hand on Jem's fair head as he moved up beside her. 'Come along, Jem.'

'See you!'

A casual hand waved them goodbye and the car was already making its way back along the muddy track before Fern realised that she had not even thanked Scott for bringing her. Jem, beside her, waved a hand, then walked with her, apparently quite happily, across the drive towards the house. She tried, during those few minutes, to find some likeness in his chubby, childish features to the housekeeper's rather stern drabness, and found none, and yet according to Scott's initial mention of him, he was the housekeeper's boy.

Whatever the relationship, Fern felt a niggle of uneasiness about returning the boy to her when she remembered Frances Dean's tight thin mouth. It was quite ridiculous to imagine that he was ill-treated, of course, for he was well fed and certainly not cowed, only a little shy, and that was nothing unusual in children of his age.

Fern had wondered before whether Mrs Dean appeared every time she heard footsteps in the hall, or if the reception was reserved only for her. For she had never yet put in an appearance without the housekeeper coming out as soon as she set foot inside the door, and this occasion was no exception.

She came out, rubbing her hands down the sides of the print apron she wore, and she frowned quickly when she saw the boy. 'Jem!' He went to her and she turned him swiftly and pushed him in through the kitchen doorway, shutting it firmly behind him. Her eyes when she turned back to Fern had a vaguely shifty look, Fern thought. 'I thought it might be Mr Barton back,' she told her, and turned abruptly back into the kitchen.

Fern shrugged. She was a curious woman and she did not begin to understand her. After nearly a week, she was no more friendly than she had been on that first occasion, and shrugging resignedly Fern opened the office door and went in. She was turned to close it when she saw Roy coming in through the front door and it was automatic to wave a hand—in contrast to his housekeeper, Roy was very friendly and she had no fear of being snubbed.

'You're back early!' He smiled and ran his hands through his hair. 'I've been down to see Caleb, he seemed a bit lame in one leg this morning, but I can't find anything wrong, so maybe he'd just picked up a stone.'

By now Fern was used to at least two thirds of his conversation being concerned with horses, and she smiled as she sat down at her desk. 'It's just as well,' she said. 'You'd hate to have to miss your morning ride, wouldn't you, Roy?'

'Oh, it wouldn't come to that!' He gave her a shrewd, narrow glance as if he suspected some intimation in her question. 'I still have Amos—it would be Scott Redman who went without his ride, not me.'

'Oh, I see.' Goodness knows why, but she had automatically assumed that the horse Scott rode was his own.

'I wish you rode, Fern.' Roy's slight frown gave the statement more seriousness than it warranted, she thought, and she smiled at the inevitability of it—sooner or later he always came back to the same question. 'I'm sure you'd love it if you tried.'

'I really don't think I would,' she denied, for what she thought must be the fiftieth time. 'And you'd rapidly lose patience with me if you tried to teach me; you've no idea how awkward I can be.'

'I don't believe it!' He came across and leaned with his hands on her desk, his eyes dark and serious. 'I can't imagine you being awkward or clumsy in anything you did.'

'I assure you I am!'

His solemn compliments were a regular part of their conversation, and Fern was beginning to get the uneasy feeling that he was much more serious about it than she wanted him to be after barely a week in his employ. As usual when he made remarks like that she sought to make light of it because she felt it was the best way to keep things from getting too serious without appearing to mock him.

'You've no idea how clumsy I can be, Roy. You wait until I've been here a bit longer, then you'll see!'

'I hope you'll be here a *lot* longer,' Roy said, as sober as ever. 'You're so much—so much more than I expected when I put in that advertisement; and you *are* happy here, aren't you, Fern?'

'Oh, yes, I'm very happy, thank you!'

'Then you must stay on.' His serious face softened into a smile that showed warmly in the brown eyes. 'You must be happy if you came back to work early!'

'Oh, I had a lift from Scott Redman, that's why I was a bit early, otherwise I'm afraid I'd have been late again.' She registered a frown when she mentioned Scott, but chose to ignore it. 'I was delayed for a while by a small trespasser in my garden. Scott says his name's Jem.'

Roy blinked at her uncertainly for a moment, then shook his head, and she would almost have sworn that by mentioning the boy she had made him uneasy, even embarrassed, although it seemed hardly credible. 'He's been to your cottage?'

Fern had no intention of treating the matter as seriously as he obviously did and she was smiling about it, making light of it as she spoke. 'Oh no, he didn't come to the cottage, I just spotted him out in the garden, wandering around the rose bed, that's all. I'm not lodging a complaint about him.'

'Just the same, he shouldn't have been down there bothering you.' He seemed determined to make something of it, and Fern already regretted telling him. 'For some reason he seems to have taken a liking to Redman, and he sneaks off down there to see him if he gets the opportunity—Redman, needless to say, encourages him. I'll tell Mrs Dean to keep a closer eye on him in future.'

'Oh no, please don't, not on my account!' She recalled the way that small solemn face had lit up at the sight of Scott Redman and hated to be the cause of depriving him of the company of his friend, however unlikely a friendship it might be. 'I like children,' she went on to explain to Roy, 'and he seems a nice lad. A bit solemn for his age, perhaps, but he's a bit shy, and I hate to be the cause of his being banned from going down there if he likes to.'

Roy, she thought, looked definitely uneasy, and there was a hint of stubbornness about his mouth that she had not noticed before. 'I can't have him making a nuisance of himself down there, Fern, and I'm not at all sure that making friends with someone like Redman is such a good idea. I'll tell Mrs Dean to keep him under better control in future.'

There seemed little point in arguing when she hadn't much grounds for arguing. Roy was the man in charge of all of them, even Scott, as his landlord, although Scott would probably deny it firmly, but she found it rather disappointing to discover that Roy could be so intolerant of a small boy's pleasures. It was a flaw in an otherwise charming character, and she wanted to see only pleasant aspects of Roy Barton.

'If you say so,' she said, but left her feelings in no doubt.

Something else that Fern had discovered during her first week in Roy Barton's employ was that almost everyone in Thorpe St Mary was either a tenant or an employee, or both, of Barton's Fen. The estate was huge, much bigger than she had first realised, and its history went back to the time of the Normans, although she could find out very little more than that, for Roy was not very keen to discuss his family history, however interested she was.

The village itself, what little she had seen of it so far, was very quiet and very English, but typical of the flat, rather secretive countryside that surrounded it, rather different from the mellow prettiness she was used to in her own county. Acres of farmland spread out like endless prairie without trees or hedges to break the monotony until the eye was caught by the soft swell of the Wolds in the distance.

Barton's Fen raised both dairy and beef cattle, but the main crop, apart from hay, was barley for sale to the brewers, and the whole business involved a great deal of form-filling as well as correspondence concerning the sale and purchase of produce. And by the end of her first week Fern had had it brought home to her just how inaccurate her first estimate of the job being fairly easy and straightforward had been.

Roy was very apologetic when he asked her to work on her first Saturday, but she was willing enough, even though she had planned to do quite a few things at the cottage during the week-end. By five o'clock she was thinking longingly of the casserole that she had left simmering in the oven, and she walked the distance down the now dry track in record time after she finished work.

Coming along the last few yards before the cottage, she spotted her neighbour standing beside his front door and frowned. Heaven knew why she should be always so unwilling to meet the man, but there was just something about him that made her so disturbingly uneasy and she seemed incapable of feeling any different.

He stood with one long leg crossed over the other as he leaned on the door jamb, and she noted, as she always did, how lean and rangy he was except for those broad shoulders under a dark red shirt. It opened at the neck and a strong column of throat emerged from its collar and merged into the first glimpse of tanned chest where the top few buttons were left unfastened. He wore blue jeans and he was smoking one of the long king-sized cigarettes he always smoked, his bright blue eyes narrowed against its drifting smoke as he watched her approach.

'Hi!' The brief transatlantic greeting was almost familiar now and she nodded a response as she came through the gate. 'Are you going to be busy for the next hour or so?'

It was a difficult question to answer without knowing what lay behind his asking it, and Fern looked at him curiously. If there was something he wanted to ask her to do for him as a favour, she felt she could hardly fail to oblige after the number of times he had offered her help. But she wished he had chosen some other time to ask, when she hadn't just finished a day's work and was anxious to enjoy her dinner before anything else.

'I was going to do something in the house after I've had my dinner,' she told him. 'Why? Is there something I can do for you, Mr Redman?'

A grimace showed his opinion of her formality, when he knew quite well that she called Roy Barton by his first name. 'For starters you could unbend sufficiently to call me Scott instead of Mr Redman,' he told her.

'Which I suspect is meant to keep me firmly in my place, isn't it, honey?'

Appalled as she was to realise it, Fern knew she was blushing, and in her embarrassment she unhesitatingly blamed him for it. 'It's meant to be normally polite, Mr Redman, and if you spoke to me simply with the sole intention of starting one of your——'

'I spoke to you because I wanted to ask you if you'd have dinner with me in Skeggy.' His eyes gleamed when he saw her look of stunned surprise; a look she was unable to do anything about because he had caught her unprepared. The inevitable grin crinkled his brown face and challenged her to refuse. 'Skeggy is the local for Skegness, if you're not yet up on the dialect. It's a drive, but it's the biggest place around here with all the lure of the big city. Will you, Fern? Have dinner with me, I mean?'

Even through the closed door of the cottage the faint aroma of a casserole cooking tickled her nostrils, and she shook her head automatically. 'I've got a meal cooking,' she told him. 'Thank you all the same—I appreciate the invitation.'

He half-turned his head and sniffed appreciatively then pulled an exaggerated face at the appetising smell from her kitchen. 'Lucky you,' he told her, and grinned an admission of the truth. 'I have to go out, to be honest. I forgot to get anything in before the shop closed—I just thought you might like to join me.'

It could simply be a ploy, but Fern was not sure enough, and certainly not callous enough to ignore the obvious solution. He did not look directly at her, but she felt sure he was watching her just the same, those blue eyes taking note of every flutter of uncertainty that flitted across her face before she took the irrevocable step.

'If you really haven't anything and you'd care to—

I've got plenty for two.' She hurried on when she saw the way he was looking at her; not exactly satisfied but certainly gratified, and she was already wondering if she had been too impulsive. A man like Scott Redman was likely to take advantage of any situation, and dining alone with him in her cottage might give him quite the wrong idea of her motives. 'It seems only fair when you've been so good about giving me lifts in your car; I feel I owe you something in return.'

'Oh now, duchess, don't spoil it!' The inevitable grin danced a web of fine lines across his brown face. 'Do I put on my best duds or come as I am?'

Fern glanced down at the short-sleeved yellow dress she was wearing and spread her arms wide. 'I'm going to stay as I am, so you'd better do the same,' she told him. 'But give me about ten minutes to freshen up, will you?'

'Take twenty, if that's what you need,' he said expansively. 'I'll be round as soon as you knock on the wall, honey!'

Nodding without saying anything, Fern opened the door and stepped inside, and when she turned to take the key out of the lock she found herself face to face with him as he pushed his head round the corner of the dividing wall. Before she had time to recover from her surprise or to realise his intent, a hard masculine mouth was pressed firmly over hers, making her catch her breath.

'Thanks, honey!'

He was gone and she was staring into space before she recovered sufficiently to slam the door hard, forgetting that the key was still in the lock. She should have known better, she told herself as she went through to the kitchen to check on the casserole. Men like Scott Redman always took advantage of every situation, and she had just committed herself to giving him dinner.

The casserole had all disappeared, followed by a hastily prepared dish of fruit pancakes with jam sauce, and Fern supposed she should feel flattered that it had all been so well appreciated. Even a man who lived on his own and cooked for himself would surely not have demolished a meal with such relish unless he had found it very much to his liking.

Leaning forward with his elbows resting on the table, he smiled across at her. 'You're going to make some lucky guy very happy one day, honey. Not only beautiful but a good cook too—it's a rare combination.'

'Thank you.'

The rather cool and distant reply was a sort of defence against the compliment because he made it sound so very sincere, and said in that deep and rather sensual voice, it evoked too many responses from her senses. But to Scott it was a rebuff and he pulled a face, his blue eyes mocking and much too close for comfort.

'Ah-ah!' he said. 'Still got the barriers up, eh, duchess?'

'Mr Redman, I do wish you wouldn't call me that!'

'While you go on acting like I'm some kind of lower order, and keep that pretty nose permanently in the air, honey, I don't see my way clear to changing it! If you'd come down off that high horse once in a while I might see you as a warm-blooded woman instead of a snow queen!'

Fern got to her feet and gathered up their empty plates, but in the same instant he was there too, standing facing her and his big brown hands taking the dishes from her unresisting fingers, shaking his head at her. She did not look up at him, for she found him much too discomfiting at such close quarters, and not for the first time that evening, she wished she had not been so rash as to invite him to share her dinner.

'I'll help with the dishes,' he offered.

She nodded her head without speaking, unwilling to object in case he saw it as yet another gesture of unfriendliness, and he carried the dishes through to the kitchen. It had occurred to her earlier to wonder why she felt as she did towards him; in fact it was a question she quite often tried to find an answer to and failed. This was not the moment to dwell on it, however, so instead she followed him through into the tiny kitchen and ran hot water into the washing-up bowl.

She showed him where the drying-up towels were and while he stood waiting for her to start washing, she was aware of him watching her; it was all too easy to imagine that faintly quizzical look in his eyes and she felt the familiar stir of resentment that blamed him for making her uneasy. She put the first plate down on the draining board and withdrew her hand hastily when he reached over to take it.

'Are you used to living on your own, Fern?'

Vaguely surprised not only by the question but also by the apparent seriousness of it, she half-turned her head to look at him. 'I had my own flat before I came here,' she told him. 'I've lived in a place of my own since I was about seventeen; ever since my mother died and my father sold the house.'

'And you like it?'

It wasn't a question that Fern had given a lot of thought to before, but she thought on the whole she did not mind the life. She had the feeling, however, that Scott Redman expected her to admit to not liking her solitary existence, though she couldn't have said why, and she looked at him briefly over her shoulder before she answered.

'I quite like it, and it means I don't have to account to anyone else for my comings and goings, as long as I don't do anything the landlord doesn't approve of. It gives me more independence.'

'And you like being independent, eh?' He laughed and the sound of it was curiously affecting in the present situation. 'Yeah, I guess you would at that.'

'Is there anything wrong with being independent?' She placed a soapy dish carefully on the draining board and didn't look at him. 'You live alone, don't you like it?'

There were dangerous possibilities in asking him a question like that, Fern realised as soon as she had asked it, and even without seeing it, she knew he was smiling. 'Mostly it suits me,' he said. 'Sometimes I think I'd like to see something a bit prettier than my own face in the bathroom mirror in the mornings, but that's something that could probably be remedied if I put my mind to it.'

It was ridiculous to colour up the way she did, and she kept her face bent over the sink in an effort to hide it from him. If she knew Scott Redman as well as she thought she did, he would appreciate the humour of seeing her blush so furiously when he mentioned changing his solitary living arrangements. With a determined effort she kept her voice cool and steady.

'Are you the only one of your family over here, or do you have a brother or sister over here as well?'

'No.'

It was something in his voice that struck her, and she turned almost involuntarily to glance at his face. He had an uncharacteristically hard look about his mouth and there was no glimmer of laughter in his eyes for the moment, so that he looked a good deal older than she had realised until now. He was probably in the middle thirties, she guessed, and this unaccustomed seriousness showed it in a way his laughter never had.

'Or perhaps you're an only one, like me?'

She had no idea why she probed deeper, except that

she found it irresistible, and he reached for another plate and dried it before he answered her, his big hands taking care not to let it slip on to the tiled floor. He did not even glance at her. 'I had a sister—a half-sister, younger than me, but she died.'

'Oh, I see. I'm sorry.'

'Yeah.'

For the moment he said nothing more and once more Fern surreptitiously studied the strong craggy features while she dried out the bowl and turned it up on the draining board. She took the tea-towel from him and hung it up to dry, then led the way back into the little living room again.

'Would you like some more coffee?' she ventured. 'I'm sorry I haven't anything stronger.'

'I'm fine, thanks.' The humour of his grin was fully restored and her own sense of relief at the sight of it surprised her for a moment. 'That was a great meal, honey, and I appreciate it.' The hasty glance she gave at her wristwatch was purely involuntary, but it was inevitable that he would notice it. 'Are you anxious to get rid of me?'

The familiar gleam of humour showed in his eyes, and Fern found it hard to find an answer that was truthful without sounding too inhospitable. In her dilemma she opted for a half-truth. 'I don't want to rush you away, but I had planned to do some jobs in the house before I go to bed tonight, and I——'

'Say no more, honey!' He held up a large hand, and his eyes gleamed vividly in his brown face as he looked down at her. 'I can take a hint as well as the next man and I don't want to outstay my welcome.'

Fern didn't want to deny that he would be outstaying his welcome in case he took it as an encouragement to stay longer, so she simply followed him to the door and

stood with him for a moment on the step. It was fresh
and cool and, at the moment, the inevitable wind was
little more than a refreshing breeze blowing in from the
sea. They were nearly half a mile from the sea, but at
certain times, like now, it could be heard in the distance.

It was not quite dark, but the moon was already
risen, fat and yellow in the clear sky, with nothing to
block their view for miles across the flat fen country
to the Wolds. Cattle were nothing more than soft dark
shadows moving in a last search for an evening meal
from the lush pasture, and the silhouettes of feathery
reeds along distant dykes swept the last daylight from
the sky.

It was the first time that Fern had appreciated the
landscape as anything other than dull and uninterest-
ing, and she sighed involunatrily as she stood with
Scott Redman and listened to the sea. 'It *is* peaceful,
isn't it?'

'Sure is!' He looked down at her, cocking an ear to
the distant murmur of sound, and he smiled. 'Hear the
sea?' His voice was lower pitched than it usually was,
and softer too, Fern thought, feeling a curious tingling
in her blood as she listened with him.

'I haven't even seen the sea yet.' She made the admission with a hint of a smile. 'It's one of the things
that will have to wait until I have more free time from
putting the cottage in order.'

It was only to be expected that he made a mockery
of her priorities, but she took less exception in this
instance, probably because she felt much as he did at
heart. 'It's only twenty minutes' stroll,' he told her. 'Not
very time-consuming!'

He must know what a temptation he made it sound,
she thought, and there was a hint of uncertainty in the

way she shook her head, though she stuck resolutely
to her decision for the moment. 'I must get this place
straight first.'

'Oh, what a virtuous maid you are!' He whispered
the words mockingly and as if he quoted them, then
once more cocked a quizzical brow at her. 'Do you
swim?'

It was inevitable, she thought, what was coming
next, but she nodded for all that, and he smiled. 'I do,
when I have the time.'

'There's always time for having fun, honey, all work
and no play applies as much to Jill as to Jack, you
know.'

'No doubt,' Fern told him, with a hint of her more
usual tone. 'But I don't have as much free time as you
do, Mr Redman.'

'Damn it, don't you like the name Scott?'

His moment of impatience startled her enough to
make her blink, but he was smiling again a second
afterwards and shaking his head. 'It's quite nice,' she
allowed, bowing to the inevitable.

'Then unbend just enough to use it, huh?'

A lopsided smile was irresistible, she found, though
she wished she had not been rash enough to linger out
here with him; he was too persuasive and this still,
quiet evening had a strange kind of effect that touched
her senses and aroused responses she was not altogether
happy about in the present situation.

'All right,' she agreed.

'And you'll make time to come swimming? Mere
Creek is quiet enough so that you think you're on
your own private beach. Unless you prefer the madding
crowd?'

Vivid blue eyes darkened by the evening light invited
her to choose, as if it was a matter of immediate im-

portance, and gave her no chance to be evasive. 'I like it quiet,' she said.

From the way he smiled it was obvious that she had answered exactly as he expected her to. 'Then I'll introduce you to Mere Creek as soon as you can tear yourself away from your chores,' he promised.

'Thank you.'

He pressed something hard and cool into her palm. 'In the meantime I guess you'd better have this!' She gazed down at the key in her hand and remembered that she had been about to take it out of the lock when he had reappeared so unexpectedly and kissed her. Since then she had forgotten all about it. 'I had thought of keeping it,' he confessed with a grin, 'but on second thoughts I figured it wouldn't do me any good.'

Flustered in a way she could scarcely conceal, Fern curled her fingers tightly over the key and tried to appear cool and controlled. 'I forgot about it,' she told him. 'Thank you.'

He had turned to face her and he was looking down at her in a way that made his intention quite clear, but somehow Fern found herself unable to make a move to stop it happening. He pulled her round and her vision was suddenly limited to the dark craggy face below its thatch of fair hair, then his mouth fastened on hers and she was conscious of nothing but the hard, rapid pulsing of her heart.

The lingering warmth of his lips was almost more disturbing than the hard pressure of his kiss, and she opened her eyes slowly to find him smiling at her. 'For my dinner,' he said in a voice that was so soft and quiet that she barely heard it. 'Thank *you*, honey.'

She said nothing, but as soon as his hands slid from her arms she turned quickly and went into the cottage, closing the door carefully behind her and turning the lock from inside. Leaning for a moment against the rough wood planks, she listened to the sound of the adjoining door closing, and then to him whistling as he made his way into the kitchen, and he sounded very pleased with himself.

It had been a mistake to ask him to share her dinner, and she must make sure she did not do anything so rash again. She could not afford to take chances with some-one like Scott Redman for one thing, and for another she had responded much too willingly to that disturbing kiss. Situations like that must be avoided in future.

CHAPTER FOUR

SUNDAY was the first completely free day that Fern had had since she arrived and, having got up late, she succumbed to the temptation of taking a little time off to relax after all. There would be time enough to get on with putting her new home to rights when the weather was a little less inviting than it was at the moment. She enjoyed walking and she had so far seen very little of her new surroundings.

It was gratifying too to discover that she had been right to assume that the countryside would look much different when the sun was shining, and much more attractive. She could not allow that it was pretty, for she missed the softening effect of trees and hedges that grew in abundance in her native county, but Roy had assured her that more of both were to be found only a little further inland.

There was no sign of her next door neighbour when she left the cottage, and she was thankful for once to have escaped his apparently tireless vigil. It was very quiet in there too, although she had heard sounds of movement earlier on, before she was up, so possibly he had gone out for the day. Anyway she had other things to think about this morning than Scott Redman, and she meant to enjoy her walk.

After a week of filling out Ministry forms she recognised the grazing cattle in the fields along the road as Lincolnshire Reds, and although their solid brownish-red colour was less attractive to her eyes than the more

familiar breeds, they had the same tranquillising effect
on the landscape as they cropped the rich pasture.
Half-grown spring lambs looked up enquiringly when
she passed, but the older ewes, plump with the autumn
crop of lambs, did no more than flick a cold blue eye
and continue with the business of eating.

A field of ripening barley skirting the road rippled
like a vast brown-green ocean in the wind, while seagulls
and lapwings cried and wailed overhead in a scribble
of whirling wings against the sky, and the reeds in the
dykes rustled with the activity of buntings and sparrows
as well as various little ground creatures like voles and
harvest mice. It wasn't so bad, after all, Fern thought
as she made her way to the village, in fact she might
even settle down quite happily in time.

The village of Thorpe St Mary itself began with a
couple of small cottages not unlike her own perched
beside the barley field, and then suddenly there was no
more stony lane and narrow footpath, but a paved
street and more houses. A church, a school and a public
house, all the ingredients of a community set in the
heart of this flat, quiet countryside.

It was quaint rather than pretty, and it was rather
bigger than she expected, with two other winding roads
leading off the main one. There were a couple of shops
and even a branch of one of the big banks along the
main street and the houses were a jumble of ancient
and modern, the older ones having that same curious
design in the front that Barton's Fen had, with the tall,
angled arch.

As it was Sunday the shops were closed, but she
peered into the windows and made a note that she need
not go far afield for most of her domestic shopping. The
church was early Norman and stood back from the
road a way, surrounded by a cluster of trees, which
feature alone set it apart from the rest of the buildings,

a squat, square little building of pale stone, patched here and there with ancient brick, and its crumbling memorials half submerged in overgrown grass. She would come back to it, Fern thought, when she had seen the rest of Thorpe St Mary.

Old churches interested her and this one had an air of mellow solidity that was very attractive, as if it was determined to survive no matter what toll time and the elements took of it. She was about to cross over the road on her way back, when she noticed someone coming down the path, leaving the church, and she frowned curiously when she recognised Scott Redman.

It was the wrong time of day for there to be a service finishing, and she thought he was unlikely to have gone to church dressed as he was, even in this more liberal day and age. He wore dark grey trousers instead of the more usual jeans, but his shirt was crew-necked and cream with a pattern in blue, and he wore it under a blue sports jacket that was swinging open as he walked. He looked very serious and he was apparently far too preoccupied to notice her among the shadows on the other side of the road.

He had parked his car just beyond the church gate and facing away from her, and he got in and drove off while she was still crossing the road, so that she frowned after him curiously. He could have any number of reasons for visiting the church apart from the usual one, but his being there somehow aroused her curiosity and she watched while the car turned the corner at the top of the main street and headed off in the general direction of Barton's Fen.

She found the church door open when she ventured to try it, and as she walked inside she was struck at once by the chill mustiness of stone walls and ancient hymnbooks, a timeless and unchanging combination. There was the usual cloying smell of age about it too, that was always to be found in old churches, and that curious flat silence that made her feel as if she was being watched.

The altar was away to her left and she realised after a moment or two that the sense of being watched was in this instance not purely imagination, for a man was coming down the aisle towards her as she ventured inside—obviously the rector, for he wore a dark cassock that swished along the ancient and uneven stone floor as he came, and a clerical collar showed as a thin white band around his throat.

He smiled as he approached, although he looked frankly curious too and obviously saw her as a sightseer. 'Good morning, are you just looking around or can I be of service?'

Wondering if she might be intruding, Fern shook her head. 'I was just looking,' she told him. 'I'm rather interested in old churches. If it's all right for me to——'

'Oh, but of course, please go where you'd like to. You'll find a pamphlet for sale on the table behind you that will tell you all about St Mary's, but if there's anything I can add——'

'That's very kind, thank you.' She bought a thin two-page booklet and scanned it briefly before telling him her identity. 'Actually I've just moved into the district and this is the first time I've been into the village itself.'

'Ah!' His expression suggested that he knew all about her arrival. 'You'll be the young lady who's come to work for Mr Barton at the Fen.'

'That's right, I arrived just a week ago—my name's Fern Sutton.' She pulled a face and recognised the efficiency of the village grapevine with a rueful smile. 'Word gets around, of course. I suppose in a place as small as Thorpe St Mary there isn't much goes on that doesn't get noticed?'

'That's true as a rule.' The existence of the grapevine was admitted without embarrassment. 'But in this
case Mr Barton said you were expected when I saw him
last.' He extended a hand and was obviously intent on
making her welcome. 'I'm Roger Maybury, Miss Sutton
—welcome to Thorpe St Mary, and St Mary's church
in particular.'

'Thank you, I'm pleased to be here.' She looked
around the tiny church with undisguised interest and
her eye was caught by a stone plaque on the wall nearest
the door, the name Barton and the date, 1850, clearly
decipherable. 'I see there are Bartons buried here—
but they would be, of course, wouldn't they? They're
a very old family.'

Obviously the local history was one of the rector's
favourite subjects, for he beamed enthusiasm. 'Indeed
yes, Miss Sutton, there were Bartons here first in Norman times, though they were known then by the
original name—de Bartrand. Only time and an English
penchant for mispronunciation reduced it eventually
to Barton.'

'Ah, I see.'

Fern's interest was genuine and, recognising a fellow
enthusiast, the rector was prepared to enlarge on the
theme. He suggested that she might like to see the older
parish records that showed some of the original de
Bartrands, and Fern was ready to agree, as long as she
did not hinder him for too long, she said, and he dismissed the idea with a wave of his hand.

'No, no, I have plenty of time before the next service,
Miss Sutton, if you would care to see some of the
records, they're in the vestry.'

It was incredible to think of these ancient docu-
ments stored away in wooden drawers and in some
cases not even locked away, and she went through the
story of the Barton family for nearly four hundred

years, tracing them back by their births, marriages and
deaths. Not concerned with later entries, she concen-
trated on those of historical interest, and she noticed
how often a titled name appeared.

The rector, apparently with the facts at his finger-
tips, confirmed that the estate did indeed carry a title
with it and had done so for several hundred years. 'The
present holder is unfortunately an absentee landlord,'
he confided, with a grimace that expressed his dis-
approval of the situation. 'Sir James married an Italian
lady some years ago and has apparently acquired a
taste for the Italian way of life. Mr Barton is an excellent deputy, of course, and has the interests of the
tenants very much at heart; he is a cousin of Sir James'
and they are in fact very much alike in appearance.'

'I had no idea.' She laughed, thinking how ordinary
she had thought the set-up at Barton's Fen originally.
'I'd thought of Barton's Fen as just a farm when I came
here first.'

'It is much more than that, Miss Sutton, indeed it
is.' The rector shook his head solemnly. 'Barton's Fen
is a vast estate and there is a great deal at stake for our
Mr Barton should Sir James die without leaving a
family. He is the nearest male heir.'

Fern tried to imagine Roy, so sober and industrious
and working so hard for his cousin's estate, his future
inheritance depending on whether or not his cousin
died childless. No wonder he took it all so seriously! A
swift and not quite undetectable glance at his wristwatch reminded Fern of how much of his time she had
taken up and she pulled a face as she checked her own
watch.

'I find it all absolutely fascinating,' she said, closing
the book she had been poring over, 'but I've taken up
an awful lot of your time, Mr Maybury, you've been
very good—thank you.'

'Oh, you're most welcome, Miss Sutton—a fellow enthusiast, eh?'

'I had no idea I'd moved into the middle of history,' she said. 'I shall enjoy my new job even more now I know how long Barton's Fen has been in existence.'

'It's quite amazing how much interest is aroused these days in family histories,' the rector told her as they walked back along the aisle to the door. 'By an odd coincidence you're the second person this morning to take an interest in our records, although the last visitor preferred to make his own way through them. I couldn't allow him access to some of the older ones, naturally, without supervision, but he seemed much more interested in recent events. Possibly he is tracing a family link with Thorpe St Mary.'

Fern was reminded of Scott's departure from the church immediately before her own arrival, and she wondered what his interest was in old parish records, for she had no doubt it was him that the rector meant. There could not be so many visitors to this little out-of-the-way church.

'I noticed Mr Redman leaving as I arrived,' she ventured. 'Mr Scott Redman—was he your other visitor, Mr Maybury?'

He hesitated slightly, she thought, and then smiled. 'You know Mr Redman, of course. He lives in the cottage next to yours, doesn't he?'

'That's right, we're neighbours.'

He had neither confirmed nor denied her speculation regarding Scott Redman's visit, she realised, but there was benevolent speculation in the friendly eyes for a moment as he shook hands with her. 'It's been a great pleasure meeting you, Miss Sutton; I do hope this won't be the last time we see you here.'

'You've been very patient and I'm grateful. Goodbye, Mr Maybury.'

'Please remember me to Mr Barton!'

Fern left the church still conscious of the rector's watching eyes, and she wondered what exactly he was thinking. Maybe he thought that she too had some other interest than the obvious one in the old records of Thorpe St Mary, but she was too preoccupied at the moment to trouble herself too much about his opinion.

For some reason she found Scott Redman's interest intriguing, more intriguing than she cared to admit at the moment, and she mused on it as she walked back home. Perhaps the rector's assumption that he was tracing his family was correct, but she could not help thinking there was something more to it than that, though she had absolutely no reason to think so.

Another glance at the time as she neared Barton's Fen reminded her of just how much time she had spent in the church, and she had meant to leave herself time to cook lunch when she got back; as it was there would be little time to prepare anything more than a sandwich. Nothing loath to wait until evening for her meal, she told herself that that was one of the advantages of having her own home—she had no one else to please.

She had opened the door and was just stepping over the threshold when she heard the sound of a latch being raised on the neighbouring door. 'Hi, Fern!' She thought he appeared slightly flushed, and she wondered why, until she noticed a tea towel wrapped around his lean waist like an apron; obviously he had been busy in the kitchen.

'Hello, Scott.' It was quite ridiculous to suggest that she felt shy with those bright blue eyes on her, and yet she could think of no other word for the way she felt and it was disconcerting to say the least. 'I've been into the village for a walk.'

'Oh yes?'

It was in her mind to tell him that she knew about his

search through the parish records, but somehow she could not bring herself to say anything; almost as if she knew he had not wanted her to know. And she looked at him curiously when he leaned round the dividing wall and sniffed noisily.

'I don't smell a Sunday roast,' he said. 'You don't fast on Sundays, do you?'

'No, of course not!'

'But you don't have anything cooking?'

Puzzled by his curiosity, Fern frowned at him. 'I went out and didn't prepare it before I went,' she told him. 'I was longer than I intended, so I'll have to have my big meal tonight—it doesn't really matter.'

It was amazing how observant she was of his expressions, and she noticed the way his eyes crinkled at their corners and the curiously crooked tilt of his mouth when he smiled. 'Does pot-roast tempt you? With potatoes and beans?'

It took Fern a moment or two to realise that she was being invited to dinner, and there was virtually nothing she could do but accept. It was so unexpected and she had not even the excuse that she had a meal already prepared for herself. Then it occurred to her how automatic it was for her always to turn down any kind of invitation from him and, as always, she was puzzled by her own reaction.

Asking her to share his dinner was simply a neighbourly gesture that she should have accepted without a second thought. Instead she was prompted by instinct to shy away from every friendly overture he made that was likely to bring them into closer and more personal contact.

'It doesn't appeal to you?'

His voice prodded her back to consciousness, and Fern smiled automatically. 'Oh yes, it sounds very good.'

'Good!' He gave an exaggerated sigh of relief that was meant to be noticed. 'I had visions of you turning up your pretty nose at my bachelor cooking. I'm glad you're not biased.'

'I don't know what makes you think I would be,' Fern told him, trying to look as if nothing had been further from her mind, and Scott grinned amiably.

'Ten minutes?' he suggested.

'At least.' She looked down at the dust on her shoes and put a hand to the havoc that a brisk breeze had played with her hair. 'I'll need to tidy myself up first.'

Sweeping over her with a swift, bold gaze, Scott smiled, and made her feel curiously vulnerable suddenly. 'No need to as far as I'm concerned, honey, you look fine.'

'Thank you, but I'd rather, nevertheless. It won't take me many minutes.'

'Take all the time you need, it won't spoil.' He was still wearing the cream and blue shirt and grey trousers she had seen him in earlier, and he glanced down his rangy length with a smiling grimace. 'Am I fit to dine with the vision you propose turning yourself into?' he asked. 'Maybe I'd better put on something more Sunday-go-to-meeting, huh?'

'No, of course you needn't,' she denied swiftly. 'I'm not going to change, only make myself a bit more presentable before I accept an invitation. After all, I've walked into the village and all round it this morning, I'm hardly in a fit state to sit down to dinner with anyone with dusty shoes and my hair looking like a bird's nest.'

A large hand reached out and the long fingers buried themselves in the silky dark softness of her hair, curling slightly so that she was aware of a gentle pull on her scalp. 'It looks gorgeous,' he said with the inevitable grin. 'But I guess being a woman you'll feel better if you stick a comb through it and tidy it up.' He let her go, heaving himself away from the door jamb, and half turned to go inside. 'You have ten minutes, duchess, so make it quick!'

He was gone and the door pushed to, though not closed, before Fern could raise objection to that derogatory nickname he had for her. She was on her way upstairs to her bedroom when she heard the familiar light baritone raised in song; the lyrical strains of a romantic ballad performed with all the fervour of an operatic tenor, and it was impossible not to smile.

The pot-roast, Fern had to admit, was as good as anything she could have produced herself, and she did not hesitate to say so when she caught her host's enquiring eye on her as he got up to clear away the plates after their first course. Her father had often cooked for himself in the days before he remarried, but somehow she had not seen Scott Redman as the domesticated type and his culinary skill surprised her.

'That was very good,' she told him. 'I enjoyed it very much.'

'And you're surprised to find that I can cook!' It wasn't a question but a statement, because he was so sure of her opinion, and Fern made no attempt to deny it.

'I am rather,' she admitted. 'I hadn't seen you as the type to cook and keep house, quite frankly.'

The bold grin he sent her suggested that he knew exactly what type she saw him as, and he laughed as he went through into the kitchen. Coming back with a glass bowl in each hand, he put down a helping of stewed plums and custard before her, then took his own seat opposite, looking across at her as he held his spoon poised in one hand.

'How'm I doing so far?'

Fern tasted the plums, then nodded approval, her eyes bright with irresistible laughter. 'Very good,' she approved. 'I compliment you on your prowess as a cook.'

'You think I could get a place with some sexy dowager as an *au pair*?' he asked, and Fern wasn't sure whether to laugh or simply ignore the implication.

'I thought you were a writer,' she said, and he shrugged, giving his attention to his food rather than looking at her.

'On and off,' he said, without enlarging on his meaning.

Nothing more was said for several seconds and Fern mulled over the situation, that only yesterday would have seemed unlikely. She felt at ease with him for the moment, and she had somehow not expected to, but then she remembered something that had not even occurred to her until now, and she sat with her spoon poised, looking across at him with narrowed eyes.

'You said last night that you'd forgotten to get anything in for your meal,' she reminded him, 'that was why I gave you dinner last night. Now today you produce roast beef and vegetables and you invite *me* to dinner. And it's Sunday, you couldn't have gone shopping since last night!'

It was too much to expect him to feel discomfited simply because she had caught him out in a lie, she realised, for he was not a man to be that easily troubled by his conscience, and she felt suddenly and quite inexplicably hurt as well as angry to think that he had fooled her. He was looking at her with bright gleaming blue eyes and getting on with his dessert as if he had nothing to account for at all.

'That bothers you, does it, duchess?'

'I don't like being lied to and made a fool of any

more than I like that—that stupid name you give me!'

It wasn't the ideal time, perhaps, to be so aggressive. Not when she had just eaten an excellent meal in his house, and he had been such a good host. But she resented being made a fool of, yet again, and she felt sure that was the explanation—there just couldn't be any other. The fact that she was so close to being angry seemed to make him wary, but there was no sign of regret in his manner, only a suggestion of seriousness when he looked at her for a moment before he replied.

'I could lie and tell you that I got the beef in Skegness or somewhere else along the coast,' he told her, 'but I won't. Seaside shops open on Sundays in the season, you know.'

Puzzled by his tangled logic, Fern simply shook her head. 'I don't think you're making sense,' she said, and he smiled.

'I'm trying to tell you, honey-girl, that I could put you firmly in your place by pointing out that I *could* have gone shopping for today's dinner, then what would you say, Fern?'

Slightly bemused, Fern looked at him for a moment, then shook her head. 'I didn't know the shops were open; I'm s——'

'Don't say you're sorry, please!' He placed a long firm finger on her lips and pressed lightly, his eyes smiling and just a little rueful, she thought. 'I just couldn't figure a better way to get to know a pretty girl who insists on turning up her nose at me than to get her to cook me a meal, honey. I played on your soft heart, and it was worth any twinge of conscience I felt at deceiving you.'

'I doubt if you have a conscience!' Fern put down her spoon with a clatter on the plate, disturbed by his apparent determination to get to know her better. 'I don't see why you have to go to so much trouble and deception either; you surely don't have to take so much trouble to get to know somebody, do you?'

'No, not as a rule; I have to admit I don't.' Blue eyes gleamed at her challengingly, and she had no doubt that he would resort to almost any kind of subterfuge the occasion demanded, once he had made up his mind about something. 'But you're different, duchess, you're so darned determined to dislike me that I have to use a few sneaky tricks to get near you. It's your own fault if I lie to you—or at least juggle the truth a little. I did have today's dinner, but not yesterday's, so strictly speaking I didn't tell you a lie, even if I did kind of forget on purpose!'

'Oh, what nonsense you talk!'

'Do I?' Another spoonful of custard disappeared between smiling lips before he put down his spoon. 'Be honest, duchess, I'd never have got past the front door of your little cottage if you hadn't thought me in imminent danger of starving to death, would I?'

It was a disconcerting question to have to answer with those quizzical eyes on her, and Fern shook her head and frowned. 'I don't know,' she confessed. 'But I don't like being made a fool of, and I seem to do little else since I came here but make an idiot of myself when you're around.'

'Oh, Fern! Honey!' He reached over and took her hands before she could do anything to prevent him, folding his hard strong fingers around hers with a curious gentleness. 'You look just like——' He looked at her steadily for a moment or two, then shook his head slowly and let her go; as if he was reminded of something he preferred to forget. 'I don't for one minute believe you're an idiot, and I think you know that quite well! Now for heaven's sake, honey, take that haughty look off your pretty face and let's have coffee!'

'I don't——'

The protest was instinctive, and Scott once more leaned across and pressed a finger over her lips, his eyes crinkled in a smile. 'And don't let's go into all that again, honey, O.K.?'

Fern had decided against letting Scott know that she had witnessed his leaving the village church, or about her own interest in the Barton family history. She did mention to Roy that she had been shown the old parish records, but apparently Roy had little interest in such matters and he had merely remarked that it seemed a curious way to spend a fine Sunday morning, so that she wondered afterwards if he had been less than pleased about her interest.

During the following week she saw very little of Scott, but the rattle of a typewriter in the cottage next door suggested that he was at last applying himself to his alleged profession, though she was still no wiser about the kind of thing he wrote. One day, she thought, she would ask him about it, but not just yet. She didn't want to display too much interest, and so far he had neatly palmed her off each time.

Her routine was fairly well established by the end of the second week, and it was a relief to find that she was not required to work on her second Saturday there. Instead she set off to do some shopping in the village and to take a look at the sea at the same time. A twenty-minute stroll was all that was needed to reach the sea, according to Scott, but he had most likely timed it from his own lengthy stride and it would take her rather longer.

Her shopping completed, she followed the directions on a white wooden arrow that pointed down a tiny side street and found herself on a steep slope with steps provided for mounting the barrier of the dunes. On the other side was the sea and a coastline that was completely different from anything she had seen before, and which at first glance she decided was discouragingly bleak and lonely.

A few moments' walking along the light sandy beach, however, began to change her opinion. It was flat, just as the land inshore was flat, but the sea rolled in in tiny ruffled waves over a wide sandy beach, and she could see for an enormous distance out to sea with quite startling clarity. The huge rolling dunes gave a sense of isolation, for they hid the landward side completely, apart from an occasional glimpse of a rooftop, but there were gulls riding the waves like small white boats, and dunlins scuttling busily at the edge of the tide.

Marram grass flourished untidily on the slopes of the dunes, and bushes of grey-green, spiny sea-buck-thorn already bearing their harvest of berries that would turn to a brilliant orange as soon as September arrived. It was so deserted that Fern got the curious impression she was alone on a desert island, except that no desert island was likely to have such a boisterous east wind blowing across it and stirring the sand into a gritty barrage that made her blink her eyes against it.

With such blank emptiness spread before her the slightest movement attracted attention, and she noticed a small figure moving along the top of the dunes suddenly, having apparently come over from the landward side. It took her a moment or two to realise who it was and when she did she frowned curiously. Apparently Jem had wandered away from home again, for she could see no one with him, and she waved a hand as soon as she thought he had seen her—he was much too small to be wandering about on the beach on his own and this far from home, she thought.

He hesitated only briefly and then responded,

ploughing along through the banked sand until he was
level with her, then looking down for a second or two
before he came running down. The sand shifted under
him as he ran and he came the last few feet rolling
over and over down the steep slope to land almost at
her feet, flushed and tousled.

He was wearing heavy black shoes which were very
unsuitable for beach walking, and his grey shirt and
shorts were covered in loose sand which he made half-
hearted efforts to brush off while he stood making up
his mind whether or not to speak to her now that he
was there. It was Fern who eventually took the initiative, smiling and rumpling his sand-spattered hair with
one hand.

'Hello, Jem, you're a long way from home, aren't
you?'

He was shy, despite that touchingly solemn air about
him, and he was not quite sure what to make of her,
Fern thought. However, he nodded, and when she
turned and began walking back along the beach he
came with her, so that she suspected Scott was right
when he suggested the boy was lonely.

'Are you on your own?' He nodded without speaking,
and she smiled. 'Then why don't you walk back with
me? I only have to call at the shop in the village for
my shopping and then I'm going home. Will you come
too?'

'Yes—thank you.'

Fern smiled to herself as he fell into step beside her,
trying to match his stride to hers and keep in step. They
said little until they had collected her shopping and
an icecream for Jem, and they were passing the village
school when she looked down at her miniature escort
and indicated the building behind its spiked iron
railings.

'Is that where you go to school, Jem?'

He shook his head firmly and kicked with one toe at the edge of the kerb in a way she felt sure she should discourage, but lacked the nerve to do so. 'No, I go to St Myrtle's in Skegness.'

'Oh, I see.'

She was not of a mind to pry, for Mrs Dean would not take kindly to her interest, however innocent, she felt sure. But having confided so much, Jem obviously saw no reason not to reveal other confidences and as he walked along beside her licking the last of his ice-cream from his fingers, he glanced up at her, frowning very slightly.

'It's a—a different kind of school.' She must have looked puzzled, for he hastened to add further information. 'Mr Barton pays for me to go there because he says it's more——' He hesitated and frowned over a word that was rather more complicated than his normal vocabulary apparently. 'More suitable,' he decided at last, and Fern looked frankly surprised, though she passed no comment.

She could hardly make the remarks she had in mind to a little boy, but she was frankly curious. If Roy Barton was indeed paying for the boy's education, as he said, then it gave rise to some very interesting possibilities. On the other hand she could be doing both Roy and his housekeeper a great injustice—possibly Mrs. Dean was a widow and Roy was simply good-hearted enough to give her help with her son's education.

On the whole she preferred to believe the latter was the case, but in her heart she could not quite accept it, no matter how kind Roy was, and she wished she had not learned about it at all. Roy was her employer, nothing more, and his private life did not concern her at all; yet somehow she could not entirely feel at ease about the situation.

Having broken the ice Jem was inclined to chatter as most children will once they are sure of a sympathetic audience. He told her about what he did at school, and how he could run faster than most of the boys in his class, his favourite teacher and his best subjects in class—there was no end to his confidences now that he was started, and Fern listened dutifully as they walked along the lane back to Barton's Fen. He was a well-mannered child without suggesting in the least that he had been subdued, and she found it very hard to see him as belonging to the grim-faced Mrs Dean.

It was almost as if the housekeeper had sensed their coming, for she appeared as soon as they turned the corner into the drive. Fern had preferred to bring him all the way rather than risk his wandering off again. The woman stood on the step inside the porch, and Fern found it curious that Jem did not immediately run to her as most children would have done to their mothers.

Instead he walked all the way to the door with Fern, then stuck out his bottom lip when Mrs Dean turned him quickly as soon as she could reach him and pushed him inside even before he had time to say goodbye to Fern. Speaking her mind wasn't easy in the face of those suspiciously narrowed eyes, but Fern felt she had to say something about where she had found him so that something could be done to stop him wandering about on the seashore alone.

'I found Jem down on the beach, and I thought he was rather small to be roaming around down there, so far from home, so I brought him back with me, Mrs Dean.'

The drab brown eyes showed not a scrap of warmth, only resentment. 'You could have brought him as far as the cottages and let him come on alone,' she suggested ungraciously, and Fern's hands tightened on the handle of her shopping bag.

'I could have, but I thought he might wander off again and you'd wonder where he was.' She faced the unfriendly stare with a discomfiting sense of having done the wrong thing. 'Please don't think I'm interfering with the way you bring up your son, Mrs Dean; nothing was further from my mind.'

She saw the quick sharpness in the brown eyes, but the answer she received was no more than she expected in the circumstances. 'I can't keep an eye on him every minute of the day,' she complained, as if she was being accused of neglect. 'Now I suppose you'll be telling Mr Barton about it!'

The adjoinder was completely unexpected and Fern was shaking her head without realising she was doing it, frowning in her confusion. 'I don't see any need for that,' she said. 'He's your responsibility, Mrs Dean, and I wouldn't trouble Mr Barton with the fact that Jem was wandering about on the beach on his own— why should I?'

A sullen shrug answered her and, seeing no further purpose to be served by prolonging the situation, Fern merely inclined her head by way of goodbye and turned to walk away. She was already half-way across the gravel drive when Mrs Dean called after her, grudgingly polite.

'Thanks.'

When she turned around she saw that the housekeeper was still standing on the step, her face shadowed by the porch and looking bleak and unfriendly, and she wished she could come even half-way to understanding that grudging and ungracious character. Then she shook her head. 'For bringing Jem home? I brought him back for his own sake, Mrs Dean, I happen to like him.'

She turned once more and could already feel the freshening breeze as she neared the gateway, still conscious, as she crossed the gravel drive, that those unfriendly eyes followed her. She was turning out on to the track when she heard the door slam shut and a curious shivering sensation slipped along her spine. She would not, she decided, like to clash with Mrs Dean too often.

CHAPTER FIVE

FERN had decided not to say anything to Roy about seeing the boy, Jem, but somehow or other, while she was telling him about her week-end activities, she mentioned that she had seen him on the beach and brought him home with her. Without looking up from dusting her desk, she frowned over the situation once more, and spoke almost without thinking.

'He seems awfully young to be wandering about the way he does on his own,' she remarked. 'Mrs Dean doesn't seem to bother very much about him.'

It had not been meant as a serious complaint but merely an observation in passing, for she was in no position to complain about Jem's treatment, unless he was being ill-treated, and she doubted if that was true. But something in Roy's voice when he replied suggested that he took her very seriously.

'She does her best for him, Fern, but it isn't an easy situation. He's very well looked after and he's quite happy in his own quiet way. Maybe he does—stray, occasionally, but that's merely boy-like, and she can't be expected to be on top of him all the time.'

Vaguely surprised to find him taking it so much to heart, Fern looked up, feeling as if she was herself under attack for criticising. 'I know, Roy. I wasn't exactly criticising Mrs Dean, only saying that Jem seems to wander an awful long way from home on his own, and he's not very old.'

'He's five and a half.' He seemed not only authoritative but resentful too, and she wondered why he should. 'He's probably been getting bored lately,' he suggested, 'being home with a cold; but he's back to school this week, so he'll have something to occupy him and keep him out of mischief.'

'Oh, good.' She was more puzzled than ever about his interest in the boy and she tidied a pile of papers on her desk while she considered whether or not she dared venture to mention something that had intrigued her for most of the week-end. 'Jem tells me that he goes to school in Skegness, not to the village school.'

'That's right.' From his tone it was quite clear that he would prefer it if the subject of Jem was dropped, and he came across to her desk, leaning on his hands while he regarded her with a steady earnestness—a sign that she was beginning to realise meant he was uncertain about what he was going to say next. 'Fern, are you doing anything this evening?' he asked suddenly.

It was a fairly familiar overture and she could guess what was to follow. To show that she was not at all averse to the idea, she smiled at him. 'Nothing important,' she told him. 'Nothing I can't put off until another time.'

'Oh, good; I was afraid——' He shrugged uneasily and thrust his hands into his pockets as he straightened up. 'I thought perhaps you might have some kind of arrangement with Redman.'

Fern eyed him curiously, wondering just how much he knew about her situation with Scott, and who could have told him if he knew anything at all. It was quite possible that Jem had seen them exchange visits and babbled about it quite innocently. Any such information, she thought, would be quickly passed on to Roy by his housekeeper.

'I live next door to Scott Redman, Roy, that's all.'

'Oh, I see.'

Obviously he expected more than that, and Fern

unconsciously angled her chin when she looked up at
him on the other side of her desk. 'I gave him dinner
one evening when he'd forgotten to get anything in,
and he repaid me by giving me Sunday lunch—that's
the extent of our socialising, Roy. Not that it really
matters to anyone else, but I hate to think of you har-
bouring any wrong ideas.'

'I was just hoping you weren't—well, involved. You
know what I mean.'

He looked vaguely sheepish and Fern found herself
feeling sorry for him. 'Yes, I know what you mean,' she
said. 'But Scott Redman is rather too brash and sure
of himself for my taste, Roy. You couldn't be more
wrong.'

'Then there's nothing to stop you coming back here
tonight?'

It wasn't what Fern was expecting to hear, and she
puzzled for a moment before shaking her head rather
vaguely. 'Come back here?' she queried.

Roy was smiling, probably realising that he could
have given her the wrong impression. 'Oh, I don't want
you to come back and work, Fern, nothing like that at
all. I just wondered—well, I wondered if you'd like to
come and have dinner with me here.'

'I'd love to.'

She answered him unhesitatingly, though somewhere
in the back of her mind was the wish that he had offered
to take her out somewhere instead of giving her dinner
at Barton's Fen. Inevitably the grim-faced and dis-
approving Mrs Dean would be in charge of providing
their meal, and Fern could imagine it would be done
with very bad grace.

'You don't mind eating here?' Almost as if he had
read her mind, Fern thought uneasily, and shook her
head.

'No, of course not.'

'Oh, good, then I'll fetch you about seven, if that's all right?'

'Quite all right, thank you.'

There was something else, she thought when he lingered by her desk still, and she looked up at him expectantly, her smile encouraging but curious. 'I thought perhaps afterwards you might like to look around a bit, see something of the farm. We could maybe stroll down as far as the stables and you could see the horses.'

So that was it! Fern sighed inwardly at the neat way he had found of working round to his favourite subject. He was genuinely anxious to have her to dinner, she had no doubt about that, but he also saw it as a chance to influence her to his way of thinking by taking her to see his horses. She was rapidly beginning to realise that, as far as horses were concerned, he was single-minded, and she could not forget either, that it was exactly as Scott had warned her it would be.

'Oh, Roy!'

She did little to conceal the fact that she saw through his plan, but he seemed quite happy for her to realise it and he smiled at her persuasively as he leaned on his hands, bringing his face closer to hers across the width of the desk. 'I'm sure if you got to know horses you'd lose your fear of them, Fern. Then gradually—in time, you see, you'll let me teach you to ride.'

He was persuasive, but her aversion to horses was too long-standing to be easily overcome, and she was shaking her head firmly. 'You know how I feel about them, Roy. I'd be hopeless even trying to get near one, let alone climb up on one!'

She was disappointed that he had had an ulterior motive for asking her to have dinner with him, and she once more remembered Scott's opinion; that Roy would see her not riding as a serious flaw in an otherwise desirable woman. It was an exaggeration, no doubt, but it was not entirely untrue, judging by Roy's behaviour.

Then he was smiling again and leaning across the desk towards her, his brown eyes warm and persuasive. 'Then will you just come and *see* my horses, just to please me? Please, Fern.'

Realising there was little she could do at the moment to convince him, she nodded agreement. 'All right, I'll go just to please you.' She looked directly at him and the angle of her chin was unmistakable as she met his eyes squarely. 'But you'll never get me on a horse, no matter how much you try to persuade me, Roy; I won't change my mind about that.'

There was no time to draw back, even had she been inclined to, before his mouth lightly touched hers for a moment, and she responded more by instinct than anything else by closing her eyes. 'Just as long as you come,' he whispered.

From the cottage next door the strains of a ballad accompanied the clatter of pans in the kitchen, and Fern wondered for a moment what Scott would have said if he had known she was getting ready to have dinner with Roy. Not that it had anything at all to do with him, but she felt quite sure he would have passed some comment if he had known.

She bathed and changed into a silky-soft pale blue dress that clung flatteringly to her figure, and she felt quite excited at the thought of going out to dinner again and dressing up for it, even if she was only going up to the house. She had no idea what kind of a cook Mrs Dean was, but the meal was bound to be better than her own hurried efforts.

Roy would like the pale blue dress, she decided as she looked at herself in the mirror, and she half-smiled as she picked up her handbag from the bed and went

downstairs again. Roy would have liked whatever she
chose to wear, she thought she could safely say that
without undue conceit. She only hoped he would
consider her too daintily dressed to visit the stables,
although she had little hope of it being so.

The singing from next door had ceased when she
came downstairs, and so had the clatter from the kitchen, so presumably Scott was already having his dinner, and she glanced at her wristwatch as a car drew
up outside. Without giving Roy time to get out, she
opened the door and waved a hand to him, then turned
and locked the door behind her.

'O.K.?' He smiled at her enquiringly, and she had
the curious feeling that he would not have been too
surprised to find that she had changed her mind about
going.

'You're exactly on time,' she told him, and he
nodded.

'I've been watching the clock ever since you left the
office, because I didn't want to be late coming for you.'
He gave her a brief but very serious glance before
starting the car again. 'I'd hate to keep you waiting,
Fern.'

Fern was not sure just what he said, for just as he
spoke she noticed a hand waving to her from the cottage
window next door, and she was giving Roy only half
her attention. She did not respond to the gesturing
hand, but its sudden appearance above the narrow half
curtain of lace at the window gave her a sudden insane
desire to laugh; a desire that she hastily stifled.

'You don't find it too quiet here for you, do you,
Fern?'

Roy turned the car skilfully on the narrow track
while she hastily snatched herself back to earth, shaking her head even before she spoke. 'No, of course I
don't, Roy; not so far, anyway.'

'Are you likely to?'

He seemed much too serious and anxious, so that she did her best to try and lighten the mood before it set the pattern for a very solemn evening. 'I'll be perfectly happy here while my boss behaves with such gallantry,' she promised, and laughed as she looked at him from the corner of her eyes.

'You inspire gallantry, Fern—any man would behave gallantly with you.'

Except perhaps Scott Redman, Fern mused as they drove along the track towards the house. He was the type of man who would take delight in being the exception to any and every rule for the sheer pleasure of being different. Annoyed that he had intruded into her thoughts when she was set on having a pleasant evening with Roy, she shook her head to dismiss him and thought instead about what Mrs Dean's reaction would have been when Roy told her who his dinner guest was to be.

It was always so difficult to remember that Mrs Dean was probably no older than Roy, no more than a year or two at most, although her general demeanour gave the impression of someone much older. Her permanently grim expression and her drab colouring did nothing to help her look more attractive, but it was possible that with a little care she could have been handsome if not pretty. Although someone at some time had evidently found her attractive enough to marry her, and she had had Jem.

Finding the housekeeper almost as disturbing a subject as Scott Redman, Fern snatched herself back from speculation once more and instead gave her attention determinedly to the landscape. Looking out at the cattle grazing placidly against a background of seemingly endless horizon, the distant Wolds merged into the evening sky until the dark swell of them looked like just another flotilla of cloud—a landscape that had been alien to her such a short time ago, but which was now becoming much more familiar and acceptable.

There was another couple of hours yet until dark, but the sky was already gloweringly low, with black clouds wallowing among the golden streaks of sunlight and casting deep dark shadows. It would probably rain before morning, but the evening was spectacularly ominous, and even if it rained before she got home, Roy would drive her. Sitting back in her seat, she had a comfortable sensation of well-being suddenly.

Instinctively she turned her head and looked at Roy and, as if drawn by her interest, he turned his head and smiled at her. 'I'm glad you didn't change your mind about coming, Fern, I'd have been bitterly disappointed if you had.'

Leaning back her head, Fern studied his good-looking but rather anxious profile when he gave his attention to the road once more. 'I wasn't likely to do that,' she said.

It was almost dark when they left the house, and Fern clung to Roy's arm as much for support over the uneven ground as for any other reason. Although it was obviously a situation he found very much to his liking, and he placed his other hand over hers where it lay on his arm, pressing her fingers lightly as they walked through the garden at the back of the house.

Mrs Dean had served them dinner in silence, but somehow still managed to convey her dislike of the situation without ever putting a foot wrong. Her resentment at seeing Fern dining with their mutual employer was unmistakable, to Fern at least, although Roy apparently noticed nothing amiss, or else concealed it well.

The housekeeper had watched them leave after their

meal with a narrowing of her drab brown eyes, and it
was something in their depths that gave Fern a clue
to her resentment. Mrs Dean, she suspected, felt more
than a liking for her personable employer, and she was
furiously jealous having to provide the dinner for their
tête-à-tête. If it was right, Fern could sympathise to
some extent, but it made her own position rather uncomfortable.

'Did you enjoy your dinner?'

She looked up and Roy was smiling. 'It was excellent,
very much better than I can manage.'

'Or Scott Redman?'

Fern frowned. Scott Redman was too disturbing a
subject to have brought up at this particular moment
and she slid her arm away from Roy's to walk along
alone for a second or two. 'Why bring Scott into it?'
she asked, and he glanced at her swiftly in the almost
dark, his brown eyes shadowy between their lashes.

'I'm sorry, Fern, I don't know why I did.' An arm
slid about her shoulders, hovered experimentally for
a second or two, then tightened when she raised no
objection, hugging her closer to him. 'God knows he's
the last person I want to talk about.'

'Then forget about him—I have!'

The ghostly leaves of whitebeam rustled in the twi-
light and she looked across at them with a smile. 'I see
you have some trees round you, but I suppose here
they don't impede the tractors, do they?'

'They make a wind break and I rather like them.'
He steered her between a couple of tumbledown gate-
posts and across a narrow plank bridge that spanned a
dyke. 'You'll soon get used to the openness here, Fern,
and you'll find it doesn't bother you half as much as
it does now.'

'If I stay after this trial period's over.' She looked up

at him through her lashes. 'You might decide I don't
fit in after all.'

'No, I won't do that!' The arm about her shoulders
tightened and she felt the hard pressure of his fingers
on her arm. 'I hope you'll stay on, Fern; my only fear
is that you'll decide you don't like the quiet and the
openness and leave.'

A rough track led across to some brick buildings that
she thought she recognised as stables, and she felt a
quickening of her pulse at the sight of them. Setting her
chin against being persuaded, she looked ahead, then
up at Roy again, a glow of challenge in her eyes.

'It isn't the trees or lack of them that bothers me at
the moment,' she told him, 'it's the prospect of coming
too close to your horses. Please don't expect me to be
brave, Roy, I can't be; I'm already shaking in my shoes
and I'm not even near them yet!'

His arm held her close and his smile suggested that
he was confident of changing her mind before very
long, while Fern was already realising that the pale
blue long dress had been a mistake. It was definitely
not the kind of thing to wear for walking across a
dirty stable yard in the near dark.

'I won't let anything happen to you, Fern, I promise.'

'Just the same——'

She bit back the words because suddenly they were
there and there was nothing she could do about it. Roy
walked over and switched on a light, then led out a tall
grey gelding that to Fern looked as if he stood fifty feet
tall. But he walked quietly enough with Roy holding
his mane and he pushed his nose into his hand when
he was stroked, making soft little snorting noises that
could have meant anything.

'This is Caleb.'

Fern still kept her distance. She admired the grey,
he was handsome and, so far, docile enough, but she

wasn't taking any chances. 'He's lovely, Roy,' she said
cautiously.

Roy's brown eyes tried to coax her nearer, but she
was not to be coaxed at the moment. 'He won't hurt
you, Fern. Caleb is my favourite and he's as gentle as
a lamb.' The low light in the stable showed a dark
brown, glossy creature who looked rather less docile,
and Roy followed her gaze. 'That's Amos, he's rather
more of a handful.'

'Then I don't want to see him!'

She thought she heard Roy sigh deeply, and remembered once more what Scott had told her. It was quite
likely that she had just gone down in Roy's estimation,
but she couldn't help that. 'I was hoping to persuade
you to come a *little* nearer to Caleb than that,' he told
her.

It was chastening to be thought such a coward, and
Fern never liked avoiding things simply because she
was nervous, even if her fear was a genuine one. Roy
waited patiently, gently stroking the grey's muzzle and,
after a few seconds, Fern moved ever so slightly nearer.
Nothing happened and she took another step, then
suddenly, on the other side of the dyke, something white
moved jerkily in the near darkness, and Caleb shifted
his hindquarters nervously, snorting his dislike.

Almost as startled as the horse, Fern stepped back
hastily, caught the heel of her shoe in her long skirt and
fell sideways on to the hard ground. Her startled cry
alarmed the animal even more, so that for a moment
Roy had all he could do to hold him, and he could do
nothing to help Fern. Stunned and breathless on the
ground, Fern saw Mrs Dean advancing with a white
tablecloth in one hand, and a bright and unmistakable
gleam in her eyes as she approached Roy.

'Excuse me, Mr Barton, but Sam Murton's on the
phone for you.'

She made no move to help Fern to her feet, but turned back to the house with an unmistakable swing in her walk that told its own story. Roy first soothed the grey until he settled, then came to help Fern, anxious and apologetic as he drew her to her feet.

'Oh, Fern, what can I say? I'm so sorry, I don't know what came over him, he's as quiet as a mouse usually. Are you hurt?'

'I don't think it's serious.' She looked down at her dress, the delicious pale blue creation she had been so sure Roy would like, and felt like bursting into tears, for the skirt was streaked with the unmistakable mess from a stable yard, and torn at the back where her heel had caught in it. If Mrs Dean had set out to ruin her dress and her evening she could claim success. 'I'd better go home, Roy, I need to get out of this dress,' she said.

'Just stay there for a second!'

She stood staring down at her dress while he hurried Caleb back in to his stable, then came back and took her arm. Looking up at him, she pulled a wry face. 'I suppose it serves me right for wearing something like this when I knew I was visiting stables,' she told him. 'But I dressed primarily for a dinner date.'

'I'm desperately sorry, and I'll replace the dress, of course; it's the least I can do.'

'It will probably clean, though the cleaners aren't going to like the job—it smells disgusting!'

'I'm sorry.'

He was obviously so contrite that there was nothing to do but exempt him from blame, and she smiled at him ruefully. 'It wasn't your fault, Roy, you weren't to know that Mrs Dean was going to wave the table-cloth to attract your attention.' She looked after the shadowy figure of his housekeeper, rapidly disappearing in the gathering dusk. 'Hadn't you better go and take that call that's waiting for you?'

'It can wait!' He dismissed the caller impatiently and gave her his whole attention. 'Did you say Mrs Dean was waving the tablecloth?'

'To try and attract your attention, I presume.' She suspected more than that, but was disinclined to say so at this point. 'It looked like a ghost in the dark and Caleb was as startled as I was.'

'Fool of a woman!'

His harshness surprised her and brought an unexpected and completely inexplicable twinge of sympathy for the housekeeper. 'She probably hoped she could attract your attention without having to come all over here,' she suggested, and Roy frowned.

'She's been around horses long enough to know better than that,' he declared, and took her arm again, turning her in the direction of the plank bridge over the dyke. 'I'll take that call, Fern, and then run you back to your cottage. Damn the woman!' he exploded as their feet thudded over the thick planks. 'She's spoiled my evening, and yours too!'

He said little while they walked back through the gardens, and Fern thought this morose and rather surly side of him was unexpected. Roy was a charmer, and charming men weren't supposed to become bad-tempered when things didn't go right for them. Scott Redman, she mused, as they went in through the back door and past the kitchen, would have laughed at the situation, and she wondered if she would have any more readily accepted that siuation.

It was only five minutes later that Roy opened his car door and helped her out with a hand under her arm, and he walked to the door with her rather as if he expected to be asked in. Perhaps she could have let him come in for a few minutes, but she was anxious to get out of the blue dress and into something that smelled a little more sweet, so she simply thanked him for her dinner and for bringing her home, then let herself in.

'I'll see you in the morning,' he told her.

'Yes, of course, Roy.' Laughing, she pulled a face. 'And I hope I'm a little more presentable by then! Goodnight, Roy.'

Ignoring the mess it must have left on his suit, he took her in his arms for a moment and kissed her—not passionately, but with an anxious fervour that suggested he was trying to make up for what had happened, and Fern wished she could respond more willingly. She was not accustomed to being in the state she was in when she was brought home from a date, and it wasn't easy somehow to get into the right mood in the circumstances.

'I am sorry, Fern, and I will replace the dress, I promise.'

'There's no need!' She had a hand on the latch and she smiled up at him. 'I don't blame you at all, Roy, but I shan't feel right until I get out of this dress and have a bath.'

'Goodnight.' He bent once more and pressed his mouth to hers, lingering for a moment, his hands at her back and drawing her lightly towards him. 'Goodnight, Fern.'

By the time she had had a bath it was nearly half-past ten, and Fern saw no point in dressing again, so she put on the pretty cotton dressing-gown she had bought before she came away, and went downstairs to make herself a cup of coffee. There was no sound from next door, but while she sat curled up in an armchair the catch on the door jiggled suddenly up and down, and a fist banged hard on the thick wooden planks.

She hadn't turned the key on the inside and she

thought she knew who the caller was, but it might be as well to make sure before she invited whoever it was to come in. Uncurling herself reluctantly from her chair, she walked over to the door on bare feet, her cup of coffee in her hand and her dark hair falling loosely about her face.

'Hi, duchess!'

Her guess had been right, but what surprised her was the fact that she felt almost glad to see him. 'Come in, Scott,' she invited.

She had forgotten for the moment that she was hardly dressed for receiving visitors, especially men of Scott Redman's calibre, but it was too late by the time she realised and he was already in through the door and closing it behind him. Turning to face her, he took note of the thin cotton robe and of the bare pink feet that peeped out from below its hem, then he smiled.

'Cosy,' he observed. 'Did you go like that to have dinner with the lord of the manor?'

Aware of how close she was to blushing, Fern turned her back on him and went back to tuck herself in her armchair once more. 'You know I didn't, because you saw me from your window when Roy came for me. I was ready for bed when you knocked—what did you want, Scott?'

She wished her voice sounded a bit more steady, for the way it trembled slightly suggested that he was having an effect on her, and she did not like to admit that. She especially disliked the idea of his possibly recognising it and finding it amusing. He stood beside her chair and she was alarmingly conscious of his being there; of the aura of warmth and virility he seemed to have which she found horribly disturbing in the circumstances.

'Apart from the reason I *could* give you, honey, I wondered if you had a jar of coffee I could borrow.'

It was the effect of his being there that made her so prickly, she knew, and there seemed nothing she could do about it. 'Don't you ever do any shopping?' she asked, and Scott laughed, perching himself on the arm of the other armchair where he could see her better, relaxed and confident.

'I forgot, duchess. I've been working, in case you hadn't noticed.'

'I heard your typewriter going the past few days,' she allowed. 'I suppose with your kind of work when you get carried away you do forget things.' She took another sip from her cup and made no attempt to get up from her chair. 'I think there's a spare jar of coffee in the kitchen cupboard—help yourself.'

'Thanks!' He might almost have known his way around her kitchen as well as she did herself, for he was back within seconds carrying a jar of instant coffee and grinning triumphantly. 'Now I shan't have to have tea in the morning. I'll pay you back, of course, coffee being the price it is.'

Her own brew smelled so good as the steam drifted up into her face that she wondered if she was being inhospitable in not offering him some, or if it would be foolhardy to invite him to join her in the circumstances. Impulsiveness was becoming an increasingly frequent part of her character lately, and she looked back over her shoulder at him.

'If you want to you can make yourself a cup now and join me,' she told him, and he did not answer for a moment.

'Honey-child——' He came and sat on the arm of the chair again, facing her, looking at her with those vivid blue eyes that gleamed and were infinitely disturbing for the things they suggested. 'You shouldn't invite strange men to drink coffee with you at this time of night, and with you in your——' Once more that all-

embracing gaze swept over her slowly and explicitly.
'Oh, I'd better go, duchess, before I get ideas above my
station!'

'Scott, for heaven's sake!'

She felt strangely edgy and refused to believe that it
was excitement that churned so furiously in her
stomach as she held her cup tightly enough to put the
thick china in danger of cracking in her fingers. Then
he bent suddenly and dropped a kiss on the top of her
head. 'You think I wouldn't?' he asked, the warmth
of laughter in his voice.

'I just wish you'd stop talking to me as if I'm not
old enough to know what I'm doing, that's all!' She
shook back the thick mass of dark hair from her face in a
gesture that was unconsciously defiant, and she knew
he was watching her with an intensity she could feel
like a physical touch. 'You'd better go, Scott!'

'Did something go wrong, Fern?' He watched her
narrowly and made no move to do as she said, even
though the initial idea had been his. 'What happened
up there, honey?'

'Nothing happened!' She was not going to tell him
about falling down in the stable yard if she could help
it, although he knew there was something wrong, obviously. 'I had dinner with Roy and then we—talked,
although I don't know why I'm telling *you* what we did;
it has nothing at all to do with you!'

Surprisingly he looked much more serious than she
expected, and it puzzled her for a moment. 'You were
home kind of early and he didn't linger long,' he
pointed out. 'I figured something must have happened
to break it up.'

Fern shifted uneasily in her armchair. Tucking her
feet more closely under her, she sat with her head bent,
gazing into her coffee instead of looking at him. 'I just
came back early, that's all, and you have no right to

keep a check on my comings and goings—I don't like it!'

Unperturbed, Scott watched her face as she sipped from her cup, and she found it disturbing being under such close scrutiny. 'I figured maybe he'd been stepping out of line.'

She glanced up, her face flushed and rashly careless of what she was saying because she felt strangely uncontrolled suddenly. 'What would you do if he did, Scott? Come to my rescue? Save me from a fate worse than death?'

'Yes, damn it, I would!' He got up from the arm of the chair and his savagery was so unexpected that she stared at him with blankly stunned eyes. 'You might figure yourself for a self-sufficient modern Millie, but you're not as self-sufficient as you like to think, I'd bet my life on it, and I——' He ran a long hand through his hair and shook his head, grimacing over his own lack of control. 'Oh hell, what am I poking my oar in for? I guess you know how to take care of yourself!'

Too shaken for the moment to find anything to say, Fern held her coffee cup tightly and tried to do something about the rapid and urgent way her heart was beating. 'I do, Scott, but——' She shook her head and looked up at him. 'I'm grateful to know that I could call on you if I needed to—honestly I am.'

'Yeah, sure!' He sat down on the chair arm once more and rubbed a hand over the back of his head, the familiar grin in evidence, though less mocking than it more usually was and perhaps even a little sheepish. 'I guess I'm old-fashioned, honey, I figure girls need a man around to take care of 'em, but that kind of demolishes the idea of independence, doesn't it?'

'But it's rather nice, all the same.'

She was smiling and did not altogether realise just how small and dependent she looked at that moment, half buried in the big armchair, and Scott was looking at her with his eyes shadowed by their lashes, his expression inscrutable. Then he shook his head slowly and got up from the chair, walking over to the fireplace and standing with an arm spread along the width of the old stone mantel.

'Why *did* you come home so early, Fern?'

For a moment her senses rebelled against telling him that she had come to grief in just about the most humiliating way possible, but it was something in that steady and challenging gaze that persuaded her eventually. Taking a long drink from her coffee cup, she emptied it, then set it down carefully, pushing her hair back behind her ear and keeping her lashes lowered.

'Roy took me to see his horses, and something startled one of them.' She did not add that Mrs Dean had been responsible for spooking the big grey, or that she suspected it had been deliberate. 'I jumped back and fell— caught my heel in my long skirt and fell over.'

'You're not hurt?'

His anxiety was genuine, she recognised, and shook her head. 'No, I wasn't hurt, but it—well, it wasn't exactly clean in the stable yard and I was——'

'Oh no!' His reaction was inevitable, but even so she clenched her hands tightly when a brief upward glance showed the brilliance of laughter in his eyes. 'Oh, honey, you didn't land slap-bang in the muck, did you?'

'Yes, I did, and it wasn't funny!'

She glared at him indignantly for a moment; she had known he would laugh if he knew about it, and she had been right about him. His tanned face was crinkled and creased with laughter and it gleamed in his eyes until they shone with sapphire brightness. Then suddenly she began to be infected by it, to see it from his point of view, and the laughter bubbled up inside her.

It shone in her eyes as it did in his and ran through her with a joyous warmth, softening her mouth and putting a flush of colour in her cheeks as she looked up at him.

'Oh, you're—you're——' Laughter welled up and overflowed, and she sat clasping her arms, hugging herself with the warmth of laughter. 'It wasn't a bit funny at the time, Scott, it really wasn't!'

'But it is now, eh, honey?'

Leaving the mantel, he came and leaned over her with a hand on each arm of her chair, his face close to hers and the vivid blueness of his eyes filling her vision when she looked at him. His eyes swept slowly over her face and she felt the hardness of his hands on her arms, drawing her up from the chair to stand close to him, a curious and infinitely disturbing smile on his mouth as he brought it closer to hers.

'You look beautiful when you laugh,' he whispered. 'You should do it more often.'

It was instinctive to close her eyes, and his mouth touched hers with a lightness that shivered through her like an electric shock, before he kissed her harder and more urgently. His hands held her arms so tightly that she wanted to cry out that he was hurting her, only she could do nothing but yield to the sensation of excitement that tingled in her blood, and press closer to the rangy length of him, taut and hard as steel.

'Scott.'

She stepped back when his hold on her arms eased, and knew that he was watching her, though she doubted if he was laughing now. Neither of them said anything more for several seconds, then Scott reached out a hand and stroked its long fingers down her face, pulling down the full softness of her lower lip before he drew back.

'I'd better go,' he said quietly, reaching once more

for the jar of coffee he had borrowed. 'Goodnight, honey.'

'Goodnight.'

She followed him to the door and he turned on the step and smiled at her, one brow cocked and a rueful downcurve to his mouth. 'I guess I just blotted my copybook, huh?'

Fern said nothing. Gathering the long skirt of her dressing-gown in one hand, she stood holding the latch ready to lock the door, and after a moment he turned to go, tossing the coffee jar carelessly into the air. She heard him open his door and his whistle as he walked into his cottage.

'Goodnight, Scott!'

' 'Night, honey!' She thought she heard a soft chuckle just before both doors closed and the keys turned in the locks—and somehow she just wasn't sleepy any more.

CHAPTER SIX

FERN slipped a jacket on over her short-sleeved dress, for there was a definite touch of autumn in the air now and it could be quite cold on the sea front. Walking on the beach had become a habit with her ever since her first venture, and it was one of the things she would miss if she moved back inland. Not that there was much likelihood of her doing so at the moment, for her job at Barton's Fen was going very smoothly, even allowing for Roy's persistence in trying to interest her in his beloved horses.

It seemed hardly possible that she had been there getting on for a month, for the little cottage was very much a home from home to her now. Even her relationship with Scott seemed to have stabilised in to a pleasant state of amiable tolerance. Never since that evening when she had taken an ignominious tumble in the stable yard and then found herself in Scott's arms being kissed had he made another move towards being other than neighbourly.

He laughed at her often, but she accepted that as inevitable, just as she did the fact that he kissed her occassionally with a careless abandon that suggested he simply liked kissing pretty girls. She accepted him as he was with a tolerance that sometimes surprised her.

It had surprised her to discover that he had moved into his cottage only a couple of weeks before she arrived herself, but his typewriter seemed to have been busy lately, so apparently he had settled in at last and

got down to some work. Whatever it was he wrote
with such diligence was still a mystery, for oblique
questions met with nothing more than a careless shrug
and words to the effect of 'this and that', which gave her
no clue at all.

The evenings were shortening and the cottage had
a cosiness she had not anticipated, once the light was on
and the curtains drawn over, but it gave her a curious
sense of comfort to know that Scott was only just on
the other side of the wall. Not that she was actually
nervous, but those miles of flat open country had a
strangely secretive air when the light was dying and
flights of homing rooks threaded their way through the
evening sky. And once it was dark the silence was complete.

The wide sandy beach, hemmed in on one side by
sweeping dunes and on the other by the infinity of the
North Sea rolling in over the flat coastline, had an
irresistible fascination for her and she tried to go there
as often as possible. Week-ends were her favourite time
because she had more time to spend and Roy was
usually occupied on Saturdays, but Scott was now so
busy himself that he had said nothing more to her
about swimming at Mere Creek.

In a way Fern was disappointed, but she had told him
that she hadn't the time and he had presumably taken
her at her word and settled down to his own work. She
had been swimming, although she so far had no success
in finding Mere Creek, so she had made do with the
available beach and found no fault with it.

Today she was simply walking, and she shaded her
eyes against the glare of the sun on the water as she
watched the dunlins at the water's edge, darting swiftly
after their prey with their curiously scuttling run that
left tiny feathery lines on the wet sand. But something
else caught her eye suddenly and she narrowed her

gaze to pick out Jem's small and solitary figure right
at the tide's edge and so preoccupied that the ruffle
of creamy foam occasionally washed right over his feet
without his even noticing it.

She was used to seeing him in grey shorts and a shirt,
but he was still recognisable in a pair of blue jeans and
a blue shirt, and oblivious of everything but what he
was doing. He had a long stick in one hand it took
Fern a second or two to realise that he was sailing a
toy boat; a scrap of white sail that fluttered in the brisk
breeze and a bright red shiny hull no bigger than a
soap-dish bobbing on the outgoing tide.

'Jem!'

It was automatic to call out to him when she saw
him lean far out to hook the toy boat back with his
stick and turn it, but the tide was against him and he
almost lost it, so that he did not look up at her, even
if he heard her.

'Jem!'

This time he bent and retrieved his boat, holding it
in one hand while it dripped water down the side of
his jeans before he looked across at her, watching her
as she made her way down the wet dark sand to join
him. He skipped back hastily when the water lapped
around his feet once more, but his eyes were bright and
slightly evasive, as if he suspected he was going to be
scolded.

'Hello, Miss Sutton.'

His black plimsolls were already soaking wet and
stained with salt water and so were the bottoms of his
jeans, and Fern shook her head at him. She had no
authority to scold him herself, but she felt sure he
would be in trouble when he got home if he got any
wetter, and she did not like to think of him being pun-
ished for being boy-like.

'Why don't you take your shoes off, Jem, and roll up

the legs of your jeans?' she suggested. 'Then they won't get wet.'

He looked down at his feet and frowned. 'I'm not allowed.'

Nor, Fern suspected, was he allowed to come to the beach on his own, although this was the second time she had found him there lately. 'Are you allowed to get your shoes wet?' she asked, trying to be reasonable from Jem's point of view. 'And your jeans—just look at you!'

The boat still dripped down his jeans as he looked down at the state of his lower half, but he gave her a brief, defiant look after a moment that challenged her authority. 'They'll dry,' he assured her confidently, 'and I'm not very wet.'

'Just the same,' Fern suggested persuasively, 'don't you think it would be a good idea to walk back with me? You've only just got over a cold, haven't you; what do you think your Miss——' she hastily recalled the name of his favourite teacher without having to hesitate too long, 'Garfield would have to say if you were away again so soon?'

Jem was reluctant to give up his game, it was clear, and Fern was in a quandary, trying to decide how insistent she should be. It was such a relief to spot another familiar figure on the vastness of the deserted beach that she heaved a sigh of relief when she saw him. A man on horseback, tall and fair and unmistakable— Scott would know just how authoritative he should be and she hoped he would see them.

It was the first time she had seen him riding and his mount was the brown gelding that Roy had described as rather a handful, but Scott seemed to have him well in hand. An unexpected thrill of pleasure rippled along her spine when she first caught sight of him, and for the moment she forgot about Jem and watched Scott ride along the beach towards her.

At first the animal came at a walking pace, stepping daintily over the rippling edge of the tide while his rider relaxed in the saddle, but as soon as Scott caught sight of her she saw the backward sweep of his heels and the horse leapt forward into a gallop, throwing up a wake of sand and water and leaving deep dark prints in the tidal mud. The animal's mane streamed out in the brisk wind off the water and Scott's tall figure bent slightly as he kept control without hindering his mount's natural turn of speed, then within a few feet of her they checked, and Fern responded automatically to Scott's inevitable grin.

He didn't wear the conventional garb, as Roy did for riding, but a pair of jeans and a white shirt that contrasted stunningly with his brown face, and he slid down to join her almost before the gelding had come to a stop, Fern stepping back hastily and automatically at the animal's proximity.

Recognising her nervousness with another brief grin, Scott gave Jem a wink, then fell into step beside her as she started along the beach once more. 'Taking your daily hike?' he asked. He caught her glance in the direction of his mount, walking just the other side of him, and he laughed. 'You're not still scared of horses, are you, Fern? I figured Roy Barton would've cured you of that by now.'

Touchy as always about the subject of her nervousness, Fern frowned at him. 'I haven't been near the wretched things since that one evening, and I don't intend to if I can help it.'

'Since you landed in the——'

'There's no need to keep reminding me, Scott!'

It seemed the most natural thing in the world for

him to put an arm across her shoulders as they walked,
and he hugged her very briefly as he laughed. 'Sorry,
duchess, I don't mean to rub it in, but you can't in all
fairness blame poor old Caleb because you fell over
your own dainty feet, can you? Be fair, honey!'

'I just don't like horses, and I doubt if I ever will!'

The arm about her shoulders tightened once more
and the vivid blue eyes glittered tauntingly at her.
'Coward!' he mocked, and turned to call to Jem.

Fern heard him swear softly under his breath and
the arm on her shoulders was snatched away as he
dropped the reins and ran back the way they had come
while she blinked in confusion for a moment. Turning to see what had distracted him so urgently, she saw
him bending over the small ominously still figure of
Jem; crouched in the frothy edge of the tide and lifting
him into his arms while the little red boat with its white
sails went bobbing away on the outgoing tide.

'Jem!'

She went racing back over the wet sand as Scott
carried him higher up the beach to where it was drier,
and laid him down carefully. Jem had his eyes closed
and there was a red mark on his forehead that suggested
he had been struck with something, and her heart
seemed to have stopped beating for a second or two
as she knelt down beside him. If she hadn't forgotten
all about him, he would have been walking with them,
and she felt awful at the moment, for letting the proximity of Scott put the boy out of her mind.

'Is he all right? What happened, Scott?' She was
appalled to realise how close to tears she was, and her
hand trembled when she touched Jem's cheek. 'It was
my fault, I should have made sure he was with us; I'd
already told him he must come back with me and then
I didn't keep my eye on him and make sure he came.
Oh, Scott, he *is* all right, isn't he?'

'He won't be any better for you flapping like a wet hen, honey.' Large and apparently competent hands explored Jem's forehead, and she watched them anxiously. 'There was a lump of driftwood down there and I guess he tripped over it when he reached for his boat, then hit his head on the thicker end, but I think he's only stunned.' He glanced across at her and looked reassuringly confident. 'If you'd strip off that wool jacket, honey, we'll wrap him in that. It's not much, but it's all we have and he's wet through; we don't want him getting a chill.'

'Yes, of course!' Fern struggled hastily out of her cardigan and handed it to him, helping him wrap it round Jem's arms and shoulders, and while they were doing it, Jem opened his eyes. 'Jem?'

She smiled encouragingly, but Jem looked first at Scott and then at her, and then started to cry. 'You're O.K., feller, you've just given yourself a crack on the head, but you're O.K.' He was gathered close in strong brown arms and cradled like a baby while Fern sat back on her heels and looked at them, feeling strangely tender towards them both suddenly.

'We'd better get him home,' she suggested after a few seconds. 'He's soaking wet and the wind's getting a bit chilly now.'

'Sure we'll get him home, eh, Jem?' He stood up with Jem in his arms still, and looked at Fern for a moment. 'Look, honey, I can't carry both of you, so I'll ride back with Jem and then come back and find you. O.K.?'

'Oh, I'll be all right, you needn't come back for me!'

Her objection was automatic and she hadn't really stopped to think what reason he had for coming back to her, but Scott gave her a very obviously resigned look as he carried Jem back to where Amos waited impatiently, and she hurried to keep pace with him.

'Sure you will, duchess, you're an independent little
nut, aren't you? Well, I won't undermine your independence by telling you that I was thinking more
along the lines of you liking my company on the walk
home, don't worry!'

'Oh, Scott!'

He put Jem into her arms while he remounted and
she forgot her fear of his horse for a moment while
she handed the boy to him once more, but she could
scarcely believe it was resentment she saw in his eyes
when he looked down at her—not Scott. Shaking her
head as he gathered up the reins, she tried to find words,
but he looked so tall and almost awesome mounted on
the big gelding that she didn't know quite what to say.

'I didn't mean it to sound like that, Scott; I'm sorry.'

'Sure!' He settled Jem more securely in the crook of
his arm, then put his heels to the animal's flanks, calling over his shoulder to her as Amos responded. 'So
long, duchess!'

'Scott!'

He wouldn't hear her, she knew it, but she had not
wanted to give him the impression he obviously had.
She would have welcomed his company on the walk
back home, even if it had meant his horse coming along
too, but he was not likely to believe it now, and she
started along the beach once more feeling very much
as if she had been misjudged.

She was still treading sand from her shoes on to the
pavement in the village street when a car pulled up
beside her, and she turned curiously to see who it was.
'Miss Sutton, can I offer you transport as far as the
lane?'

Bending to see who the driver was, she smiled when
she recognised the rector of St Mary's. 'Thank you, Mr
Maybury.' She got in beside him and smiled gratefully.
'I don't usually bank on riding back when I go for a

walk, but I'm rather anxious to get back today.'

'Oh?'

He was only mildly interested, she could tell, but she saw no reason not to tell him. 'I saw little Jem Dean on the beach,' she explained, 'then Mr Redman came along and I took my eye off him for just a moment, and in that time he tripped and hit his head on a piece of driftwood.'

'Oh, my goodness!' He looked startled, and she realised how dramatic it had sounded in the telling. 'Is he seriously hurt? Is a doctor necessary?'

'Oh no, I'm sure it won't be!' She smiled reassuringly, hoping she was right. 'He's bruised his forehead, but he seems all right apart from getting soaking wet; Mr Redman's taken him home.'

'Ah, yes, I see.' He seemed confident of Scott's ability to deal with the situation. 'A very capable man, Mr Redman.'

He glanced at her briefly, and Fern wondered just what she was expected to say in reply. In fact she simply nodded agreement. 'So I believe.'

'I believe I saw Mr Redman on horseback earlier; I imagine that's how you come to be making your own way home, Miss Sutton, eh?'

His smile was a little too meaningful to be comforting and Fern hastily avoided his eyes. 'Scott—Mr Redman took Jem with him on his horse, but I'm anxious to get back and see how he is.' She recalled Mrs Dean's stern features with discomfiting clarity and sighed. 'I do hope he doesn't get into too much trouble from his mother for being down there on the beach on his own.'

The brief silence that followed was no more than a few seconds' duration, but to Fern it seemed loaded with meaning, and she glanced curiously at the man beside her, wondering what she had said that caused it. 'You know the child's mother, Miss Sutton?'

Something made Fern cautious, almost wary, although she had no reason for the way she felt except the tone of voice in which the question was asked. 'I meant Mrs Dean—Mr Barton's housekeeper.'

'I know the lady, Miss Sutton, she's one of my parishioners, but I fear you're under a misapprehension. Mrs Dean is not the boy's mother, she simply—cares for him.'

'Oh!' Not knowing quite what to say, Fern sat for a moment with her hands in her lap, and she still had not brought her thoughts to order when the car pulled up at the end of the track to Barton's Fen. A hand on the door handle, she hesitated, half-turned in her seat. 'Are you sure, Mr Maybury—I mean——' She shook her head apologetically. 'But of course you're sure— I'm sorry.'

He took no offence at her doubt, but shook his head, half-smiling as if he understood and sympathised with her confusion. 'I've lived in Thorpe St Mary for the last fifteen years, Miss Sutton, and Mrs Dean has been coming to my church for most of that time. She was married there and her husband is buried there; her husband died seven years ago and she had no children.' He looked at her directly and it was not easy to meet such a look with the thoughts that were going through her mind. 'The boy is not yet six years old, is he?'

'No, he's five and a half.' She could hardly point out, Fern felt, that the child did not necessarily have to be the late Mr Dean's; it seemed rather uncharitable in the circumstances. Instead she opened the car door and smiled at him before she closed it again. 'I'm very grateful for the lift, Mr Maybury, thank you.'

The door of the next cottage was ajar when she arrived home and she frowned at it curiously. She expected Scott still to be stabling his horse, even though he had handed over Jem to his mother, or whoever Mrs Dean was, for she hadn't been far behind him, thanks to the rector's opportune arrival. Instead he was obviously home already.

Not only that, she realised as she walked down Scott's side of the path, but Amos, the brown gelding, was tethered to a ragged-looking shrub at the end of the cottage, nibbling Scott's patch of lawn with cautious disdain. She gazed at him curiously for a second, then tapped on the cottage door.

'Scott?'

She heard him speak to someone before he called out to her. 'Come on in, Fern, it's open house!'

It took her a second or two to adjust her vision to the darker interior of the cottage, and then she saw Jem, wrapped from head to toe in a blanket and holding a cup of something in both hands, tucked into one of the huge armchairs. He had a bruise on his forehead, but it did not look nearly so bad as she expected, and he was rosy-cheeked and not a bit pale, his blond hair rubbed dry and left uncombed, just as Scott was some-times wont to do with his own, and she could not re-strain a smile at the sight of him.

'Jem, are you all right?'

The boy nodded, and Scott got up lazily from his own chair when she came in. 'He'll survive,' he told her, grinning at his small visitor, 'but I figured he'd be better off down here than up there with that dozy female.'

'Mrs Dean?'

His description startled her. She could think of quite a few adjectives to accurately describe Mrs Dean, but dozy wasn't one of them, and she looked at Scott curi-ously. Indicating the armchair he had just vacated, Scott perched himself on the arm of the one Jem occupied and shook his head.

'Mrs Dean isn't home,' he told her in a flat firm voice that suggested he did not like the situation, 'and neither is Roy Barton. Jem was left in charge of the cleaning woman, that's how come he slipped the noose.'

'He's always slipping the noose,' Fern reminded him, and noted how Jem's bottom lip pushed out reproachfully. 'Didn't the woman know he was gone?'

'I doubt very much if she knows anything about anything,' Scott told her bluntly. 'She looked at me like I was something from outer space when I walked in with Jem, and she didn't seem like she knew what to do about him, so I figured he'd be better off back down here until somebody else comes home.'

Mindful of the bright blue eyes watching her, almost challenging her to deny that he had done the best thing for Jem, Fern nodded. 'You make a very efficient baby-sitter,' she told him. 'I see you've stripped him and dried him and given him a warm drink.'

He sought and held her gaze for a second or two until she looked away and there was a glint of mockery in his eyes. 'What did you expect me to do, duchess? Stand and flap helplessly for a female to come and tell me what to do?'

'Hardly—I've learned how self-sufficient you are already! Just the same, most single men don't know a lot about taking care of children, and you might have panicked a bit.'

'I did!' A broad grin made her doubt the admission and he rubbed a hand over Jem's blond thatch. 'But we coped, didn't we, pal?'

'I'm not a baby!'

Jem had only just realised what her term baby-sitter implied, and he was looking at her indignantly from the depths of his blanket, a situation that Scott seemed to be finding amusing, for he was laughing. At her,

Fern suspected, not at Jem, and she knew it was no more than she could expect of him.

'I know you're not a baby, Jem.' She sought to make her peace with the little boy, and getting up from her chair she smiled at him. 'I've got some chocolates in my cottage next door, would you like one?' From the way his eyes gleamed it was clear what his answer would have been, and she laughed as she turned to the door. 'I'll go and get them!'

Ten minutes later Jem had already demolished nearly half of one layer in the box of chocolates, and Fern was wondering how she could tell him that he would probably make himself sick if he ate any more, when a car pulled up at the gate and she glanced at Scott curiously. He was nearest the window, and he pulled aside the curtain and looked out, then turned and grinned at her.

'The lord of the manor!' he told her. 'I think he's coming to see you—you'd better let him know that you're visiting next door!'

The malice he managed to get into the simple sentence surprised her, although she knew as well as Scott did that Roy was not going to like finding her in his cottage. Putting down the chocolate box, she went to open the door, and Roy lowered his hand when he saw her, then cast a swift and frowning glance behind her.

'Hello, Fern. I called on you earlier, but you were out.' Once more he glanced into the cottage behind her and raised a brow. 'At least, I thought you were out at the time.'

Instinctively on the defensive, Fern stiffened. 'I was out, Roy, I've been for a walk as I usually do on a Saturday morning.' She stepped back after a brief glance over her shoulder. 'You'd better come in—Jem's here.'

'Jem?'

He came into Scott's little cottage, and with the two of them in it it seemed to shrink to the proportions of a doll's house. Jem in the armchair looked up, then hastily looked down again, and his bottom lip was thrust out in a way that suggested he was prepared to stand by his actions no matter what was said. Roy looked at the all-enveloping blanket and the smear of chocolate on his face and frowned.

'What have you been up to, young man?' he asked.

'He was on the beach, Roy, and he fell and hit his head on some driftwood.' Fern hastened to fill him in, anxious for there to be no misunderstanding. 'It's nothing serious, but he was stunned for a moment and he was wet through. Fortunately Scott was handy and he rode home with him.'

'I noticed Amos outside,' Roy observed, quiet-voiced but obviously far from pleased with the situation. 'Did you take him with you to the beach, Fern?'

'No, she didn't, pal, she rescued him, so don't try to pin the blame on Fern.' There was a quite unexpected edge of steel on Scott's lazy drawl that made Fern stare at him for a moment in surprise. He eased himself away from the mantel where he had been leaning, and walked to within a foot of Roy, facing him with a curiously disturbing half-smile on his mouth. 'That dumb female you have up there doing the dusting doesn't exactly shine as a baby-sitter and she didn't know what to do when I brought him back, so I carted him back here and stripped him off.'

Roy looked uncomfortable but still unhappy about finding her there, and he obviously had no idea that Jem had been left in charge of the daily woman. 'Wasn't Mrs Dean——'

'Mrs Dean's out some place,' Scott informed him, still

in that exaggerated drawl and watching him through the smoke from one of his long cigarettes, 'so that female with the broom told me, and she didn't strike me as being capable of taking care of a dog, let alone a kid with a sore head and soaking wet. Fern's fed him chocolates and he's had a mug of hot milk to ward off the chill, so I figure he's come to no harm.' He gave the boy a broad wink. 'Unless he's feeling sick to his stomach from too many chocolates.'

'I'm not!'

Jem was quite firm about it, and it was clear that Roy was at a loss for the moment. He seemed uneasy too, Fern thought, and she wondered why he should be so concerned with his housekeeper's son—if indeed he was Mrs Dean's boy as Scott had told her that first evening. Mr Maybury had given her food for thought on that subject.

Bringing himself to positive action suddenly, Roy walked across to Jem's chair. 'I'll take him back with me in the car and get him off your hands,' he said. 'I'll let you have the blanket back, Redman.'

'Oh, sure!'

Scott watched him with speculative eyes while he picked up the boy and carried him to the door, turning in the doorway to speak to Fern. 'Thank you for taking care of him, Fern.'

'I didn't, Scott did!' She remembered the chocolates then, and smiled. 'I gave him a few chocolates, that's all, and I only hope he *isn't* sick after them!'

It struck her how much less at ease he looked with Jem in his arms than Scott had, and when she thought about it it seemed rather odd. For Roy was the one she would have visualised as the settling down type who would become a husband and father, not Scott. He looked so serious too, and not a bit as if he understood Jem's behaviour, as Scott did.

'He really hasn't come to any harm, Roy; and he's none the worse for it, I'm sure.'

He seemed about to say something else, but he nodded instead and turned to put Jem in the front passenger seat before looking at her again. 'Thank you just the same, Fern, he could have come to worse harm if you hadn't been there.' He glanced behind her at the doorway. 'And Redman too, of course. I'll see you tomorrow, perhaps? Are you going to be busy?'

Unaware that Scott was standing just behind her, she started to shake her head when he spoke up; still using that slow drawl that somehow made her feel he was mocking the person he spoke to. 'You promised to come to Mere Creek swimming, honey, remember?'

The slow drawl and the familiar 'honey' were guaranteed to grate on Roy's edgy nerves, she knew, and she wished he was not so easily slighted. She had promised to go to Mere Creek with Scott, but that had not been mentioned again since that first time, and she would feel horribly guilty if she lied about it to Roy now. Looking over her shoulder at Scott, she met the blue eyes head on and much too close for comfort, so that she looked away again hastily as she shook her head.

'I did promise, but not for tomorrow, Scott.'

Roy looked past her at Scott, and the amount of satisfaction that showed so clearly in his eyes for a moment almost made her regret having denied the promise. 'Then I'll see you tomorrow afternoon,' he told her, and smiled for the first time since he arrived. 'Take care, Fern.' It was an act of sheer bravado, she knew, when he leaned forward and kissed her mouth. 'Until tomorrow!'

His stride when he walked round to take his seat had a confident spring in it and he waved a jaunty hand as he drove off with Jem beside him. Fern watched him go, preoccupied with the air of possessiveness he had

towards Jem, and so absent-minded that for the moment
she forgot about Scott standing just behind her in the
doorway and literally bumped into him when she
turned round.

'I'm sorry!'

Her breathless apology seemed to amuse him and he
held her arm as he led her back into his cottage, sitting her down in one of the armchairs before she
realised that she could have gone back to her own.
'Have coffee now you're here?' he offered, and she hesitated, looking up at him with a hint of uncertainty and
ignoring the invitation for the moment.

'I'm sorry, Scott.'

'What for?' He stood with his hands on his lean
hips, looking down at her with an amused half-smile
that did not quite match the more serious look in his
eyes. 'After two back-handers in one day, I've got the
message, duchess, don't worry! Strictly touch-me-not,
hah?'

'Nothing of the sort!'

The denial was immediate and impulsive, made without a thought given to the fact that it was open to mis-
interpretation, and Scott's brows quizzed her mockingly. 'No?'

'I mean I wasn't—I'm not trying to be unfriendly.'
She shrugged, knowing she was making a poor job of
explaining, but inexplicably at a loss for words. 'I know
you thought I was being stand-offish when I said you
needn't bother coming back to the beach for me, but I
simply meant you didn't have to bother about me when
you had Jem to bother about. And I'm sorry I called
your bluff about tomorrow, but I hadn't promised to go
swimming with you—not tomorrow.'

'Honey, I'm not blaming you—I should have followed through the first invitation.'

'I rather thought you'd had second thoughts since

you haven't mentioned it since,' Fern told him, wondering if she was being rash in not simply letting the matter drop.

'Not me.' Blue eyes challenged her and the smile on his mouth gave it a disturbingly sensual look. 'You say the word, honey, and we'll go—any time you say.

'I thought you were working——'

'I can always spare time to go swimming with a pretty girl!' He stood looking down at her and she felt a sudden quite startling urgency in her pulse as she hastily avoided his eyes once more. 'Now you're here,' he said, 'you *will* have coffee with me, won't you?'

Fern nodded, not at all sure she was doing a wise thing in view of that look in his eyes. 'Yes, thank you,' she said. 'Can I help?'

His sudden laughter mocked her and he dropped a kiss on the top of her head as he walked past her into the kitchen. 'A woman in my kitchen? Heaven forbid!'

He made good coffee, and Fern always suspected he had his own way of making it that made it taste so different, and they sat in the two big armchairs drinking it slowly, with a tranquil kind of silence between them that she had experienced before in his company and never quite understood. She still had the matter of Jem in mind, and after a while she spoke of it, almost without thinking about it.

'I'm never quite sure where Jem fits in somehow,' she mused.

'Fits in?' He quizzed her over the rim of his coffee cup and he was quite serious, she noticed. 'How fits in, Fern? He's Frances Dean's son, so what's to fit him in?'

'Is he, Scott?' She caught a quick narrowing of the blue eyes and wondered if she was going too fast without enough knowledge of the real facts. 'Mr Maybury denies that Mrs Dean has a child. When I referred to her as Jem's mother he corrected me; told me that Mr

Dean died seven years ago and that she had no children.'

Scott was smiling, rather sardonically, she thought, and looking into his cup from which the steam rose in thin ghostly swirls. 'Could it be that the Rev is a little—unworldly?' he suggested softly, and Fern wished it did not fit so neatly with her own sentiments.

'I thought of that,' she confessed, 'but that isn't the only odd thing that strikes me concerning Jem.' She felt rather disloyal speaking as she did, but somehow it did not seem so bad saying what she did to Scott, and there was always the possibility that he already knew, for he was friendly with Jem, more so than she was herself. With that in mind, she stilled her conscience. 'Did you know that Roy pays for Jem to go to a private school in Skegness, Scott?'

Eyes narrowed, he looked at her for a moment with no sign of the usual laughter, and she noted once more how much older he appeared whenever he was very serious. Then he laughed shortly and took another sip from his coffee. 'You *have* been busy, haven't you?' he mocked. 'Who told you that, honey?'

'Jem.'

He considered for a minute, then conceded the possibility with a grimace. They sat in silence for a while until he looked across at her again, and his eyes were still serious, slightly narrowed and penetrating enough to make her feel he could see right through her. 'So what did you deduce from that, Fern, eh?' She didn't answer, because she suspected she did not need to, and after taking a cigarette and lighting it, he blew smoke across the intervening space and eyed her through the haze. 'You're thinking young Jem might be Roy Barton's, huh? And you don't like the idea!'

'I'm not saying anything of the sort!'

She denied it hastily and Scott was smiling, a crooked,

mocking smile that held little humour. 'Oh, come on, honey, at least have the courage of your convictions!'

'All right, I *don't* like to think it about Roy, but even if it's true, it has nothing to do with me—or you,' she added, unable to resist the taunt. 'I wish I hadn't said anything to you about it, now.'

'Yeah, I can imagine you do, honey, but you did, and you've got me speculating now. It's possible, I guess, though I don't go for the Reverend's theory that Jem can't belong to Frances Dean because her husband died seven years ago. I guess maybe I take a more critical view of human nature!'

'A more cynical view!'

The blue eyes had a bright, glittering look that mocked her own suspicions, and he laughed. 'Pot calling the kettle black, duchess?'

'Yes. Yes, I'm sorry—I'm as bad as you are, because I can't believe it's as impossible as Mr Maybury says either. But I just can't see Roy—I can't believe that if Jem was his as well as Mrs Dean's he wouldn't have married her.'

His smile mocked her, but it did not, she noticed, reach his eyes. 'Honest, upright Roy Barton, eh?'

'I think so, yes!'

'You've known him—how long is it, Fern? Less than a month, and you can be that sure of him?'

'You haven't known him much longer, and it doesn't matter how long I've known him, Scott! I think Roy's a decent man and I think if Mrs Dean had had his child he would have married her!'

'And maybe you don't know the Bartons that well!'

'Do you?'

For a moment Scott said nothing, but sat smoking his cigarette, a drift of smoke successfully hiding his expression from her. Shadows flitted across the darkly tanned face and made it closed and secretive, quite unlike its usual openness, so that she wondered if she knew him as well as she thought too.

Then he raised his head and looked directly at her, blowing smoke from between pursed lips, and she thought he seemed distant somehow, although she could not have explained the impression he gave her. 'Do you know anything about the Bartons, Fern? About the family, I mean?'

Fern nodded vaguely. 'I went to the church one Sunday morning between services and Mr Maybury showed me the old parish records. I'm interested in things like that, and so is he, apparently, we had quite an interesting hour or so.'

A smile flitted briefly across his mouth, a mere ghost of his usual grin. 'And I've spent hours in the local pub,' he told her. 'Did you know that Roy Barton's only the manager of Barton's Fen?' She nodded and he looked vaguely surprised for a moment. 'Sir James Barton is the owner, but nobody around here likes talking about him much; absentee landlords, understandably enough, aren't very popular, and Sir James lives abroad.'

'Yes, I know, he——'

'Well, did you also know that if the present title-holder dies without an heir, our Mr Barton stands to become Sir Roy?' The vivid blue eyes held hers relentlessly while he drove home his point. 'You can see what I'm getting at, can't you, Fern? Can you imagine the stir it would cause around here if the new Lady Barton was his lordship's ex-housekeeper? What the local bigwigs would have to say about it?'

Fern could all too easily imagine it, but she was not yet prepared to condemn Roy without having a good deal more to go on than she had at present. 'Roy isn't a snob, Scott, not to the extent that you imply, I won't believe it!'

'Well, maybe I'm wrong, I'll be the first to admit it if I am, but I don't see how you can be so darned sure that he isn't a snob!'

'Can you prove he *is*?'

Fern was on her feet without even realising she had left her chair and she faced him angrily when he got up too, reaching for another cigarette and looking more resigned than angry, she realised resentfully. He was regarding her with a kind of resigned tolerance that she found infuriating in the circumstances, though she was thankful that at least he wasn't finding her defence of Roy amusing.

'If he *is* Jem's father,' he said quietly, 'isn't that proof enough, wouldn't you say?'

'And if he isn't?'

His eyes had a darkly absent look that she did not remember seeing there before and she watched him closely while he smoked his cigarette. 'If he isn't, and Mrs Dean isn't Jem's mother as the Reverend says,' he told her in the same quiet voice, 'then I'll be very interested to know who is.'

There was something about him that she found strangely disturbing suddenly, and Fern shook her head. 'I don't think I want to know,' she said. 'And I've got quite a lot to do, Scott, so I'd better go. Thank you for the coffee.'

'Yeah, sure.'

He was still standing beside his chair and drawing deeply on his cigarette when she went, and he merely waved a vague hand when she turned in the doorway, apparently much too preoccupied to even notice her going, and she shrugged uneasily. It wasn't like him, Fern thought as she unlocked her own cottage door, and she wished she did not feel it mattered so much.

CHAPTER SEVEN

FERN found the subject of Jem slightly embarrassing now that there were so many doubts about his actual identity, and when she had asked after him the day following his accident on the beach, Roy had been very evasive, merely giving her a stiff and very brief answer, as if he would prefer the matter closed.

She felt sure Scott was convinced the boy was Mrs Dean's son, if not Roy's as well; for herself she preferred to leave Mrs Dean's role as it had always been to her knowledge, and regard Roy's interest as simply that of a kindly man who felt sorry for a child under his roof. He did not have to be personally involved, she told herself repeatedly during the following week, he was simply being kind.

For some reason Scott seemed to have abandoned his typewriter again lately and went out a good deal more, and for several mornings now the cheerful voice in the bathroom next door had been silent. It was difficult for her to understand, but Fern not only missed his singing but was troubled by its absence, and she even thought of asking him the reason for it.

She had been rather preoccupied lately with one thing and another and inevitably Roy was bound to notice sooner or later. He did not spend a great deal of time in the office now that Fern knew the ropes, but when he was there she came in for the majority of his attention, and it was impossible not to recognise a growing seriousness in his attitude towards her.

He came across to her desk where she sat filling out

forms, and leaned on his hands, bringing his face quite close and looking at her for a moment before he said anything. It was inevitable, she knew, but she sighed inwardly when she anticipated the interruption and wondered if she would get the lists of figures transcribed in time.

'You look rather cross,' he remarked, and she looked up to see him smiling rather uncertainly.

Brown eyes searched her face anxiously; Roy invariably looked anxious, she had noticed, and she sometimes wondered what made him so uncertain. From her own knowledge of the accounts she knew he had nothing to trouble him where the financial state of the estate was concerned, so it could not be that which gave him his air of concern.

'I'm not cross,' she denied, smiling to prove it, 'I'm just concentrating, Roy. I'm filling in the quarterly returns and I always feel somehow as if I'm dealing with people who don't speak the same language as the rest of us.'

'Yes, I know what you mean!' His eyes warmed and he leaned closer, then reached out and stroked a forefinger down her forehead between her brows. 'I don't like to see you frown, Fern, you're much too pretty for that, and especially over anything as mundane as Ministry returns.'

'It's what I'm paid for—remember?'

A flutter, strangely like apprehension, stirred in her breast as she looked up at him. She often wondered what she would do when Roy eventually took the inevitable step she had been anticipating for some time now. She could not pretend to be immune to his quiet kind of charm, and he was certainly good-looking, but somehow she was not yet prepared to make up her mind about how she felt about him in a more serious vein.

He simply stood there looking down at her for several moments until Fern felt he was waiting for some other response from her. Before she could summon one, however, he spoke again and once more reached out a hand to touch her face, this time tracing a gentle line down her cheek. 'You *are* very lovely,' he said in a voice barely more than a whisper. 'I wish I could put it into words, Fern—the way I feel about you; but you must have some idea, haven't you?'

It wasn't possible to just go on sitting there in the circumstances, and Fern got to her feet, escaping the caressing finger on her cheek and feeling a little better able to cope now that she was more on a level, although she still felt oddly uneasy. It shouldn't be like this, she told herself; not when a good-looking man all but told you he was in love with you; it should bring a sense of elation, surely, not cause a flutter of near panic because you didn't know what to say to him.

'Oh, Roy!'

He came round the desk to her and took her hands, holding them firmly between his while he looked down at her in a way that made a further declaration inevitable. 'I love you, Fern, I think you know that. I began falling in love with you the moment I saw you in that hotel room, when I interviewed you for the job, and now I've seen you practically every day for over a month I've no doubts at all.'

But she had far too many doubts herself, Fern thought, far more than she would have if she felt as deeply as Roy did about her. She had always liked him, but it had gone no further than that, though she hated the idea of telling him so. Instead she chose a less direct way out, and shaking her head, she looked down at the hands he held so tightly in his, rather than look at him.

'I need more time, Roy; it isn't very long, only seven weeks, and I can't——'

'No, of course you can't!' He bent his head and pressed his lips to her fingers before he released them, and his voice had a huskiness that was much too affecting for her peace of mind. 'I wanted you to know so that you could—think about it, about us. I suppose it isn't very long and maybe I've spoken too soon, but I just had to say something.'

It was such a touching little speech that Fern felt strangely sad when she heard it, but she could not in all honesty claim that she felt any differently about him because of it; it would not be fair to mislead him about anything so important. Instead she moved across to the window, then turned and smiled at him, the sunlight catching her hair and shading the darkness with a gold sheen, her gold-flecked eyes shadowed by dark lashes.

'I'm very touched, Roy, and flattered—truly.' Her own voice was slightly unsteady and husky with unaccustomed emotion as she looked across at him. 'I wish I could be as certain as you are, but I can't and I'm sorry.'

'Oh no, darling, I don't blame you!' He came across to her in long urgent strides and took her arms, looking down into her face with the familiar anxiety showing again in his eyes. 'You have nothing to be sorry about, and I promise I won't mention it again until you're more sure how you feel. Though I can't promise to find it easy working here with you and *not* saying anything.' He smiled ruefully and kissed her mouth so lightly that she barely felt it. 'I'll try and be patient, my love,' he promised.

It seemed to have been a very long day somehow, and as she walked the last few yards to her cottage and saw

Scott, Fern wasn't sure whether she was pleased or sorry he was there. He stood on the path eyeing the border of straggly marigolds that was almost his entire garden, as if he contemplated pulling them out. His back was towards her and he didn't turn around until the gate squeaked when she opened it, then the sight of his grin decided her. There was something irresistible about his grin that she was bound to respond to, and did.

'You're not thinking of murdering the last of your marigolds, are you?' she asked as she came along the path between the two gardens, and he rubbed the back of his head thoughtfully.

'What do you think?' He regarded the untidy border ruefully, as if its continued existence was of prime importance, and Fern could not restrain a smile as she stood with him.

'They're about finished, I suppose, but it seems a shame to get rid of them when they're all you've got. Do you have to suddenly decide to become tidy, Scott? Couldn't you just leave them to die in their own time?'

He turned and looked at her neat little grass patch surrounding the small round bed with its two rose bushes, and pulled a face. 'You put me to shame,' he confessed. 'I saw you weeding your patch yesterday and I thought I'd better do something about mine. The trouble is I'm not used to gardening, I've never lived in the back of beyond like this before.'

'You've called it that before,' she reminded him as he followed her along the path. Taking the key out of her handbag, she stood with it in her hand for a moment after she opened the door and smiled at him curiously. 'If you feel like that about the place, why do you go on living here?'

'For the peace and quiet, remember?' He followed

her into her cottage without waiting for an invitation, and she did not bother to remark on it. 'I wanted peace and quiet to work in.'

'Yes, I remember, but Lincolnshire isn't the only quiet place in the British Isles, you know. Why didn't you try Wales or Scotland? You should feel at home there with your name—are you Scottish, by the way? I've often wondered.'

'*Have* you?'

She took off her coat while she talked and hung it up, and Scott leaned against the edge of the kitchen door, waiting for her to come through in that direction. He grinned at her as she passed him and reached for an apron from the back of the kitchen door, handing it to her and catching her eye for only a second, just long enough to make her seek refuge by glancing at the clock on the wall.

'If I'd known you were interested in my antecedents, honey, I'd have been glad to enlighten you. I'm second generation Canadian, but my grandpappy was a Scot; one granny was French and one granny and the other grandpappy were English. Does that fill you in?'

Fern was aware that she had flushed cheeks, partly because she suspected he was laughing at her yet again, and she kept her face hidden from him as far as possible while she got on with preparing her evening meal. 'I wasn't asking for your family tree, Scott, I was simply —slightly curious, that's all.' She turned on the gas cooker and spoke without looking at him. 'And you still haven't said why you particularly chose Thorpe St Mary to live in.'

She half expected him to laugh off her curiosity, or give her some silly reason that would make her laugh, but instead he said nothing for a second or two, so that she half-turned and eyed him curiously. Catching her eye, Scott grinned ruefully and shook his head.

'I was kind of hoping you wouldn't press that question,' he said, and Fern stood with a saucepan in one hand and frowned at him uncertainly.

'I'm sorry; I told you, I'm not——'

'No, no, it's O.K., honey.'

He looked across at her with fathomless blue eyes, thick fair lashes lowered just enough to hide their expression from her. Briefly the old familiar grin appeared, then faded to a more rueful smile that hovered about his mouth as he left the doorway and came to sit on the edge of the kitchen table, swinging one long leg while he talked.

'I think maybe I should tell you why I'm here, why——' He shrugged with deceptive carelessness, then went on, glancing at her obliquely, 'Because you're the girl you are and I've seen the way Roy Barton looks at you, I figure you should know.'

Her pulses were more urgent and yet she could think of no special reason why they should be at the moment, but she got on with what she was doing because in some curious way she sensed that he did not want her to look at him. 'What's all this about, Scott?' she queried.

He shrugged once more and she guessed he was smiling that curiously rueful smile that wasn't at all like his customary grin. 'Past history, I guess, and maybe stones that would be better left unturned, only I can't somehow leave them unturned.' She would have questioned his meaning yet again, but he went on quickly before she could do so, 'You remember I told you about my sister, Fern?'

Fern nodded, doing the jobs she did automatically while she gave her whole mind to what he was saying. 'Your half-sister—you said she died.' It struck her then why he was there, and she turned and looked at him. 'She died here?'

He was still watching his own foot swinging rhythmically back and forth and he didn't look up. 'She died in Louth Hospital, according to the certificate the solicitor sent us, but she was in Thorpe St Mary only a few weeks before that, so I figured this was the place to come and find out *why* she had to die.' He antici- pated her question with a shake of his head. 'Oh, we knew the reason, but I wanted to know just what hap- pened here six years ago—that's why I'm here.'

Fern stared at him, her hands still for a moment. 'All that long ago?'

He looked up at her and smiled, that crooked, rueful smile that she was beginning to dislike so much. 'I told you it was past history, honey, but I only just found out certain things. My stepfather, Faye's father, was of Dutch origin, but he was born here in Lincolnshire and Faye got it into her head to come and look for other de Hahns.'

'And did she find them?'

Scott shook his head, still remembering, she thought, for he had a curiously distant look that was quite unlike him. 'She didn't find any more de Hahns, but she did meet someone she fell in love with. There was someone back home, someone she'd known all her life and was all set to marry as soon as she'd got this trip out of her system, but when she met this guy she was over the moon.

'All her letters had something to say about him; how great he was, how crazy she was about him. Pop wrote her to come home, she already had a decent guy back home ready to marry her, but Faye didn't want to know, she was going to marry him no matter what anybody said; and I guess I was responsible for the way she defied Pop as much as anybody was. We were kind of close, me being so much older, I guess she figured I was that much wiser.' The sudden crookedness of his smile made Fern's heart skip. 'How wrong could she be?'

'What did you tell her, Scott?'

He did not look at her for a moment, then he shrugged and shook his head slowly. 'I told her to do what made her happiest—what else would I tell her, honey?'

'Of course.' What else *would* he tell her, being Scott?

Fern went on doing things automatically, much too distracted to be conscious of anything deliberate. 'Then suddenly there weren't any more letters and I was just dumb enough to believe it was because she had found a guy who filled her whole world; and she was young, only nineteen, she didn't think about family obligations and all that junk. I didn't find out how wrong I was until Pop de Hahn died last year, and I unearthed all the letters he'd kept back.'

'She wrote to you again after she married?'

Fern stopped what she was doing and made no more pretence of being concerned with anything but what he was telling her. He looked so much older, as he always seemed to when he was very serious, and there was a tightness about his mouth, a dark bitterness in his blue eyes that showed just how deeply he still felt his sister's death whenever he allowed himself to think about it.

'Oh, she never did marry her wonderful guy, honey, he didn't want to know when it came to the marriage bit!'

'Oh, no!'

'Yeah!' His mouth smiled, but there was a steely coldness in his eyes that made her shiver. 'I guess you girls just never learn, do you? You fall in love with some guy and suddenly everything's guaranteed perfect—wedding bells and the old happy ever after. Only it doesn't always work out, does it?'

Fern could understand his bitterness to a degree, but

she hated to hear it, and she shook her head. 'She was so young,' she said. 'She must have been heartbroken.'

Scott looked as if he approved of the expression, and he nodded. 'I guess that just about sums it up, honey. Her heart was broken and she just didn't want to live any longer; that's what killed her, whatever the doc at the hospital put on the record.'

It wasn't easy to say, but Fern had to ask. 'Didn't—wouldn't she have been better if she'd gone home?' she ventured. 'Didn't she write and——'

'She wrote asking what she could do, and I didn't reply.' His voice interrupted her briskly. 'I didn't reply because Pop de Hahn in his righteous, puritan soul saw fit to cut her out of all our lives for good. Let her go her own way, he said, without once mentioning the cries for help that he pushed to the back of his desk drawer and left there for five years until I found and read them—five years too late.'

'Oh, Scott!' she sighed.

'He knew I'd have been over here like a bat out of hell if I'd got one whiff of what was going on, but I never did—he saw to that,' added Scott.

Fern felt oddly helpless, and Scott said nothing for several minutes, but reached out and took her hand in his, caressing her slim fingers, then he looked at her and grinned, though not with the same blithe impudence he usually did, and she missed that more than she cared to admit.

'So—now you know why I'm here, duchess, eh? Why it had to be Thorpe St Mary and not somewhere in Wales or Scotland. I'm trying to put the books straight, though I'm still not sure if I'm doing right, raking over old ashes.'

Fern did nothing about freeing her hand so that she could get on with preparing her meal, but realised as she stood close to him that she rather liked the warm strength of his fingers around hers. 'And have you?'

'Put the books straight?' He shrugged. 'I've made a start, honey, but I've a ways to go yet, I guess.'

'You know who the man is—was?'

Scott did not reply at once, he simply sat holding her hand and looking down at the hand he held. 'I know his name, but I knew that before I came here; what I didn't realise was how many men there are in this area with the same name and I can't put a foot wrong in anything as—delicate as this. I figure I've cut it down to a short list now, but I have to be very sure before I let anybody know who I am.'

'Faye's brother?'

Scott smiled wryly and nodded his head. 'Yeah, that's it, honey—it's going to be a shock to somebody one of these days.'

Roy had arranged for them to take a drive into the Wolds the following day; as a surprise, he told her, and seemed very pleased to have persuaded her to go with him, although Fern had in fact needed very little persuasion. She would have been happy enough to go anywhere with him, for she had so far seen nothing of Lincolnshire but the flat fields and coast around Thorpe St Mary, and she had begun to doubt that there was any more to it than that, despite the high rounded promise of the Wolds on the skyline.

The further they drove inland the more obvious it became that what she had seen so far was no more than a flat rim around a much more picturesque scene. Woods and trees bordered the narrow twisty lanes, and hedgerows sheltered all the familiar wild flowers as well as an abundance of animal life.

Pheasants strutted in the fields and an occasional, more shy, partridge, and hares loped lazily away from the roadside as they approached. It was much more

than she expected and she found it comforting somehow to know that this lush, prolific countryside was
within such easy reach. She exclaimed so often and so
excitedly at this very different aspect of his home
county that Roy turned and smiled at her.

'Are you so very surprised?' he asked, and with a
rueful grimace Fern admitted it.

'I had no idea that the outlook could change so much
in such a short distance,' she confessed. 'Yes, I *am* surprised, very pleasantly so, and I'm glad you arranged
this drive, Roy, it's been a real eye-opener.'

His expression suggested he was well satisfied with
the verdict, and he nodded with only a ghost of a
smile. 'I hoped you would be,' he said.

Shortly afterwards they turned into another narrow
lane, twisted around a couple of corners and were running alongside a grass verge that widened suddenly
into a clearing, overshadowed by tall trees. With a
brief glance over his shoulder at her, Roy drove over
on to the clearing and pulled up and, unsure just why
he should have chosen this particularly quiet spot to
stop, Fern looked at him a little warily, a faint smile
just hovering on her mouth.

'Somewhere special?' she asked, and Roy looked
mysterious.

'This is Somersby.'

Obviously she was expected to follow his meaning,
but for the moment she had no clue. 'It looks very
quiet and rural,' she said, and Roy shook his head at
her, pointing back the way they had come.

'Did you notice that biggish house just back there?'
he asked, and Fern nodded, still puzzled. 'That was
Somersby rectory.'

Still the allusion evaded her, although some small
stirring of comprehension roused itself in the back of
her mind as she looked at him and frowned. 'I have a

feeling it *should* mean something, Roy, but I just can't think at the moment.' He watched her for a moment longer, evidently enjoying her puzzlement judging by his expression, and eventually she glared at him in mock reproach. 'Don't keep me in suspense, Roy, tell me where we are!'

'You must have learned it in school,' he told her. 'Tennyson's father was rector of Somersby, Fern; the poet was born in that house.'

'Oh, of course!' She clucked her tongue in exasperation at her own slowness and laughed. 'I was never very good at English Lit. at school, so that will have to be my excuse for forgetting!'

Roy turned and got out of the car, indicating what looked like a deep dyke behind him at the other side of the clearing. 'Just down there is Tennyson's babbling brook, if you'd like to get out and have a look at it.'

'I'd love to!'

Determined to make up for her initial slowness, she walked round to join him on the bank above a disappointingly ordinary-looking stream, barely more than a trickle despite a wet summer, and looked down at it curiously. It seemed to have no special virtue as a subject for such praises as the poet had endowed it with, but she found it a pleasant enough interlude in the circumstances. It meandered peacefully and if you listened in the warm late summer silence you could hear it, chuckling softly around a fallen tree branch.

'It reminds me of a place we used to go for picnics when I was a little girl,' she said after a moment or two, and smiled at the memory that had lain forgotten until now. 'I used to sail little paper boats my father made for me from the pages of his pocket book; until they became waterlogged and sank, then I cried.'

Roy's arm was around her shoulders while they walked a little further on up the hill to a bridge that carried the road over the poet's brook, and there was a much better view from there. Fern made no move to evade his arm, for it was a drowsy summer's day with no sign of the autumn coolness they had experienced lately, and it seemed so very right to be there, walking along a tree-crowded country lane with an arm about her shoulders and a good-looking man beside her.

'Did you sail boats?' he asked, smiling down at her. 'I thought it was only boys who have toy boats.'

'Girls too,' she assured him, then remembered a small boy with a red-hulled boat that went bobbing away on the tide. 'I suppose living so close, you sailed your boats on the sea, like Jem does?'

It seemed to Fern that the arm around her shoulders became taut for a second or two, and he took time to answer her. Then he thrust his free hand into a pocket and spoke without looking at her, his voice rough-edged, as if he resented being reminded of the little boy he seemed to treat so possessively.

'Jem puzzles you, doesn't he, Fern? You—can't quite make out who or what he is, why he's at Barton's Fen, and it troubles you, doesn't it?'

His almost aggressive frankness was unexpected, and Fern already wished she had not started a conversation she felt she was bound to regret before much longer. She leaned on the parapet of the bridge, gazing down into the water and watching a leaf swirl round and round as it was borne along helplessly, out of sight, just as Jem's little boat had disappeared.

Snatching herself back hastily, she looked at Roy from the corner of her eye. 'It doesn't so much trouble me as puzzle me, Roy. Not,' she added hastily when she felt him about to speak, 'that it has anything to do with me, but you did mention it.'

'With a reason.' His arm settled about her shoulders more firmly and he leaned his head close to hers. 'I'm hoping that you'll love me enough to marry me eventually, Fern, and I don't want there to be anything that can come between us.'

'Roy——'

'No, please, darling, let me go on.' His eyes had the now familiar look of anxiety that she found so appealing in certain circumstances, and he spoke with an earnestness that suggested he was not altogether sure of being believed but was determined to be heard. 'I imagine that Redman has made a few wild guesses about Jem——'

'Not in my hearing, Roy!' Heaven knew why she had decided to come to Scott Redman's defence with such fervour, but it was clear that Roy did not like her doing it, and she swiftly averted her gaze to the running water below the bridge once more. 'I saw Jem at the window of Scott's cottage on the first evening I was here,' she explained. 'I went in to have a cup of coffee with him and I saw this little face at the window. Like an idiot I yelled as if I'd seen a ghost, because it startled me, suddenly appearing like that—then Scott told me it was very likely Mrs Dean's boy.'

'I see.'

'I had no reason to doubt it at the time and I'd still have no reason to if Mr Maybury hadn't given me a lift the day Jem hurt himself on the beach. I referred to Mrs Dean as Jem's mother and he—put me right.' She still wasn't too sure that the rector had put her right, but Roy seemed not to notice her brief hesitation. 'As I said, Roy, it doesn't concern me really.'

'It will concern you if you're going to become part of my family, as I dearly hope you will when you've had time to think about it,' Roy insisted. 'I thought you understood that Mrs Dean simply looks after Jem— she certainly isn't his mother. In fact Jem is my cousin James's son.'

Goodness knows why it startled her, but it did, and her expression probably showed as much. 'Sir James?'

Roy's eyes narrowed for a moment when he looked down at her, and she could guess that he did not relish the idea of her learning anything about his family that he did not tell her himself. 'I see you're quite well informed,' he said shortly.

A little on the defensive, Fern looked round at him. 'You told me yourself that you were managing Barton's Fen for your cousin—I haven't been prying behind your back, Roy.'

'No. No, of course not.' He still kept an arm about her shoulders, but she thought there was a slight coolness in his manner. 'I seem to remember you told me about going through the old parish records with the rector just after you came here, didn't you? I suppose he told you about James—he's an expert on the Barton family history, and it's a sore subject with most people in Thorpe, that James is an absentee landlord.'

Which was much the same thing that Scott had said, Fern thought, and she moved away from the bridge, back along the road towards where they had left the car. 'I know that Sir James is married to an Italian and lives in Italy,' she told Roy when he followed her and put his arm around her once more. 'But I was much more interested in the older Bartons than the present-day ones, Roy. I didn't bother with anything later than the early nineteenth century.'

'I hope you don't include me in the ones you have no interest in,' Roy said, and she smiled, thankful to have him restored to a better humour.

'Of course not. But I was just trying to explain to you, Roy, that I haven't been poking around into your family's more recent history; it isn't any concern of mine.'

He walked beside her, his arm hugging her close and his head bent close to hers, so that they would have looked like a couple of lovers to anyone else using that quiet country lane. But Roy was serious and a small frown tugged at his brows, as if he was still not convinced she took his intention to marry her seriously enough.

Stopping on the grass clearing, he turned her to face him and said nothing for a moment or two, but stood looking down into her face, as if he sought words. Then he bent his head and kissed her gently on her mouth, one hand cradling her chin, his brown eyes glowing with warmth.

'I love you,' he whispered, 'and I mean to marry you, my love, sooner or later.'

'Roy——'

'Does it take you so long to decide?' It was so unexpected to recognise impatience in his voice that she looked up at him swiftly and frowned.

'In something as serious as saying I'll marry someone,' she told him, trying not to sound too reproachful, 'I *have* to take a long time to decide, Roy. You wouldn't want me to say I will and then live to regret it, would you?'

'I hope you never will!'

She turned once more and began to walk back to the car, and after a moment's hesitation during which he frowned at her departing back, he came after her and once more laid an arm across her shoulders, as if to establish that right at least. 'If it's the fact of my having Jem with me that bothers you, Fern, that's quite easily settled. He's in my charge simply because James didn't want him with him, but that can soon be changed. I'm just his guardian, and not even a legal one; James is still responsible for him and I shall simply tell James that I can't be a stand-in for him any more.'

A chill shiver fluttered along the length of Fern's back like an icy finger, and she gazed at him unbelievingly. 'You'd—send him away? Just like that?'

She found it hard to understand how a little boy could be shifted from hand to hand to suit the convenience of adults, but Roy apparently saw nothing wrong in it. 'James is his father,' he reminded her. 'He was a widower when he met his present wife and he didn't want any—complications, that's all, so I agreed to keep Jem at Barton's Fen with Mrs Dean to help care for him, until he's old enough for boarding school. But if my situation changes, as I sincerely hope it will very soon, then James will have to take on his duties as his father, that's all there is to it.'

'I see.'

He sensed where her sympathies lay, she thought, but he did not altogether understand them. 'Jem won't suffer, I don't think he even realises that he's related to me—I'm not very good with children and for the most part I don't see much of him.'

Fern remembered then that Jem had referred to him as Mr Barton, and it stunned her for a moment to realise what a chill and undemonstrative atmosphere the little boy must live in; no wonder he responded so well to Scott's warm friendliness.

'Poor Jem!'

She did not think Roy heard what she said, and he was anxious to drop the subject, as he had each time before when she had mentioned Jem. Turning her face to him with his palm against her cheek, he looked down at her. 'And now can we change the subject, my love, and talk about something *much* more interesting to me—you?'

Although she was still troubled by Jem's eventual fate, Fern could see no point in pursuing the matter further at this stage, and she shrugged uneasily. 'If you really want to,' she told him. 'But I'm not a very interesting subject, I warn you.'

Roy stopped and turned her to face him once more, a hand curved about her cheek while he looked deep into her eyes. 'I'll be the best judge of that,' he said softly, and kissed her mouth.

CHAPTER EIGHT

IT was Sunday morning and Fern lay in bed feeling lazy and listening to the strains of a French love-song coming from the kitchen next door. She could identify it now; since she asked Scott what it was, and he had told her it was one his French grandmother had taught him when he was at school. Saucy, he assured her with a wink, but quite romantic.

She supposed she should be getting up too, but she had succumbed to temptation to lie abed much later than usual, thanking heaven that she had turned down an invitation to go driving again with Roy, and then to lunch somewhere afterwards. Her excuse had been that she had a lot to do around the house, having done nothing at all the day before, but in fact she had wanted some time to think over her relationship with him.

The sun came in through her window and made long black shadows on the walls, and it was a warm, still day outside, the kind of day that made her want to do nothing more energetic than sit back and look at the sky and be lazy. She didn't even want to think about her feeling for Roy with any degree of seriousness, and she was getting no nearer to a solution when a loud banging on the door downstairs startled her into alertness.

It couldn't be Roy, even if he had decided to come and see her after all, for he would never come pounding on anyone's door like that, and particularly if he thought there was a likelihood of her being still asleep. It had to be Scott, and the raised voice that accompanied a second assault on her front door confirmed her suspicion.

'Hey, Fern, are you there?' Her first instinct was to giggle, but she stifled it determinedly and pulled the bedclothes up over her head instead, muffling her ears against a further thud on the thick wooden planks. 'Fern! Are you there?'

She sighed, throwing back the covers and getting out of bed. The window was partly open and she poked her head out and looked down at him where he stood peering in through the downstairs windows. For a second or two she stood looking down at the top of his head and a pair of broad shoulders in a grey shirt; his head was bent to look in at the window and his neck was bare and brown where it emerged from the collar of his shirt. Her reaction at the sight of him from this unfamiliar angle startled her for a moment, for she felt an incredible sense of excitement, and a curious tenderness too, for the vulnerability of him in his present position.

'Good morning, Scott!'

He jerked up his head and she was looking instead into the tanned face and the vivid blueness of his eyes. Then he grinned, and the inevitability of it added pleasure to the strange chaos of emotions that whirled through her spinning head.

'Hi, duchess, aren't you up yet?' Very briefly anxiety clouded the mocking laughter in his eyes. 'You're not sick, are you, honey?'

Leaning her elbows on the window sill, Fern shook her head. 'No, I'm perfectly all right, thanks, but it *is* Sunday morning and I was coddling myself with a lie-in.'

'I hadn't seen you around and I wondered if you might have gone off before I got up. Were you asleep?'

'Hardly, with you singing French songs at the top of

your voice!' Laughter took the edge off the criticism, and she eyed him curiously. 'What's wrong? What are you doing pounding on my door as if the place was on fire?'

'It's a beautiful day, duchess!' He spread his arms wide and invited her to agree with him. 'Isn't it?'

She had to agree and she did so unhesitatingly. 'Lovely.'

Placing both hands on his hips, he smiled up at her, and even from her bedroom window she could see the laughter web of lines that crinkled the corners of his eyes. 'I just made some coffee and I thought you might like to down a mug with me before the lord of the manor whisks you off again for the rest of the day.'

'I'm not seeing Roy today, as a matter of fact.'

'All the better!' He quizzed her, arms akimbo and his feet planted firmly apart on her patch of lawn. 'Did you have a fight yesterday?'

He sounded very much as if he expected her to confirm it, and Fern frowned at him. 'No, we didn't fight—why should we?'

Still smiling, he shrugged. 'I dunno, honey, I guess I had a feeling, that's all. So what are you going to do about that coffee? Are you going to join me?'

'I suppose so.'

Laughter made a mockery of her reticence, and he shook his head. 'Such graciousness! I'll expect you in ten minutes, duchess!'

He was already half-way back to his own side of the path when Fern called after him, pushing the window wider and leaning out. 'Not ten minutes, Scott, I'm not——'

'O.K., twenty, then!' He stepped back before going into his own cottage, looked up and gave her a broad wink. 'Come on, honey, move it or the second lot of coffee'll get cold too!'

In fact it took Fern just twenty-five minutes to bathe and dress, and she was still warm and sweet-smelling from the bath when she tapped on Scott's half-opened door and went in. He took note of the light blue dress she had put on and sniffed the combination of bath essence and perfume appreciatively, coming to bend his head until his face was close to hers.

'You smell warm and sweet and beautiful,' he murmured, and slid an arm around her waist, his strong fingers pressing into her for a moment. 'Good enough to eat!' He buried his face briefly in her hair and his lips brushed her neck lightly, then he looked directly into her suddenly evasive eyes and laughed softly. 'Sit down, honey, I'll get the coffee.'

'Can I help?'

She felt curiously light-headed for a moment, and wanted to do something to restore normality, but Scott was shaking his head, his eyes bright with laughter as he went through to the kitchen. 'To make coffee? No, thanks, honey, I prefer my own!'

It was true, his coffee was always much better than hers, and within minutes she sat drinking it from a thick pottery mug, looking across at him in the other armchair. At times like this he never looked the thirty-four years he laid claim to, and she always found it hard to believe she could relax so much more easily in his company than she was able to in Roy's.

He leaned back in his chair with his long legs crossed one over the other and stretched out in front of him, and catching her eye suddenly his own were mildly curious and slightly narrowed. 'Have a good time yesterday?' he asked.

'Yes, it was lovely. We went up into the Wolds and Roy took me to see Tennyson's babbling brook. The country's so much different there from here, it was a real eye-opener.'

'And did he quote Tennyson to you?'

Suspecting sarcasm, Fern looked at him closely before she answered. 'No, he didn't, Scott, and I wish you wouldn't be—funny at Roy's expense.'

'I wasn't being funny.' Surprisingly she felt he was telling the truth. 'If I'd taken you to see Tennyson's brook I'd have found something suitable and murmured it in your ear—I'm surprised he didn't.'

'Well, he didn't!'

'Hmm!' He seemed to have sobered somewhat from his initial conviviality, and she wondered what he had on his mind as he watched her from the depths of his armchair with a slow and deceptively lazy scrutiny. 'He's pretty serious about you, isn't he, honey?'

If he had asked her the same question in his usual bantering fashion, Fern would have told him that it was no concern of his, and refused to even answer his question, but he seemed to sober himself, and his voice was deep and quiet, and curiously affecting somehow. She held her cup tightly in both hands and looked down at the contents rather than at him.

'Roy wants me to marry him.'

'Uh-huh.' His lack of surprise, she supposed, should have been unexpected, but somehow it wasn't. 'And did you say you would, Fern?'

She hesitated only briefly. 'No. I mean,' she added hastily, 'I said I needed more time to think about it, but —actually I shall tell him I can't.'

She had not known what her decision was until that moment, but suddenly she was very sure. She did not want to marry Roy, and she was sure she never would, no matter how much more time she spent thinking about it. Scott hadn't been looking directly at her while she told him, but he raised his eyes and smiled at her.

'I'm glad to hear it, honey.' He took a long drink from his coffee mug and nodded. 'Very glad to hear it.'

'Oh?' Fern's heart was thudding so hard that she felt breathless, and she held her cup tightly despite the hot coffee in it that tingled against her palms.' 'Why, Scott?'

He took another drink, then sat forward in his chair, resting his elbows on his knees. 'Mostly because he's—who he is, I guess.'

'I don't think I understand you. What do you have against Roy?'

Clasping his mug tightly between his big hands, Scott shook his head and he must have known she was frowning at him, even though he was studying his hands instead of looking at her. 'Maybe nothing,' he confessed. 'But when Faye first wrote about that guy she fell in love with, she told us his name was Barton—just that, she never used a first name for him, only referred to him as Bart from then on, and that's all I had to go on when I came over here.'

Fern felt as if she had been stunned by a blow. She had known Roy for slightly less than a couple of months, but she worked with him every day, and she had become close to him as a person too. What Scott was saying aroused too many possibilities that she was not yet ready to face, and for a moment she did not know what to say. Then she looked across at him and shook her head.

'Roy? You think it was Roy?'

Scott's broad shoulders heaved in a shrug. 'I don't know, honey, and maybe I shouldn't say anything until I *do* know, but seeing him getting so close to you——' There was a curious helplessness in the way he held his big hands, spread wide, and then he glanced up and gave her a brief and rather sheepish grin. 'I hope it isn't him, because I kind of like the guy and I don't think he's the sort of rotten so-and-so who'd treat Faye that way—I hope he isn't.'

'I hope so too.'

Fern put down her cup and twisted her hands together as she tried to convince herself that Roy would not behave as Faye de Hahn's faithless lover had. But still too clear in her mind was the way he had told her he would send Jem away from Barton's Fen if it suited her to have him go. It had struck her as an incredibly harsh attitude to take towards a small boy, but it was the kind of thing that the man who had jilted Scott's sister would do, and she found the knowledge horribly worrying.

'Scott——' She hesitated, wondering if it would convince Scott and make up his mind for him about Roy, if she told him. 'I learned who Jem really is yesterday; Roy told me.'

'Mmm?' A hint of suspicion lurked somewhere in his eyes, and she went on, still not sure that she should have told him.

'He said he wanted matters straight between us before I made up my mind about marrying him. Jem is Sir James's son by his first wife. Sir James was a widower when he met his second wife, the Italian woman, and he didn't want Jem with him when he went to live in Italy, so he left him with Roy.'

'You're sure of that?' He looked doubtful, and Fern wondered just how strongly convinced he had been that Jem was Roy's son and how reluctant he was to have to change his opinion. 'So he isn't Frances Dean's after all?'

'No, not according to Roy, and he should know, I think.'

'And?' He was looking at her closely, his blue eyes narrowed and curious, though friendly enough to invite confidences, and he smiled when she looked across at him uncertainly. 'What else is there about young Jem that worries you, honey? I see that little frown between your eyes, so I know there's something on your mind.'

Fern knew the reason for it well enough, but she hesitated to tell Scott how ready Roy had been to dispose of Jem for his own convenience. That had been a side of his character she had not suspected existed and she could still feel shocked by the easy way he spoke of it. Scott was waiting, knowing she had something on her mind, but it wasn't an easy thing to admit that someone she had thought she knew fairly well after their weeks together fell so far short of her estimation of him, and she got up from her chair and walked aimlessly across to the window.

'I know you'll think I'm too squeamish,' she told him, already on the defensive, 'but it was partly because of Jem that I decided I couldn't marry Roy, even if there wasn't the very good reason that I don't love him.'

'Because of Jem?'

She hadn't heard him move, but he was standing now by the old-fashioned mantel and lighting a cigarette, and when she turned her head to look at him his eyes were narrowed behind the rising smoke. She nodded, looking once more out of the window.

'He told me that if when I married him I didn't want Jem with us he'd——' She turned once more and looked at him with a frown between her brows, seeking his understanding. 'Scott, how could he be so ready to send Jem away, back to his father, who doesn't want him either, just to suit his own purpose? Two grown men ready to—to dump a little boy on whoever happens to be handiest, because he's a complication.' Her eyes sparkled with sudden anger. 'That's what Roy called him—a complication! Can you imagine that?'

He took a moment, then shrugged his shoulders resignedly. 'Yes, I guess I can, honey. From what I've dis-

covered about the Thorpe St Mary Bartons, being
callous comes easy; though I had thought better of Roy,
I have to admit.' He came across to her where she stood
by the window and put the cigarette he had just lit in
the ashtray beside him, while he took her by her arms
and looked down into her face. His eyes scanned the
troubled eyes and the soft uncertainty of her mouth
for a moment, then he shook his head. 'And you're so
soft-hearted, honey-girl, aren't you?'

His voice was softer in timbre than Fern ever remembered before, and a small shiver of anticipation
slid along her back when he drew her closer to him. She
felt her legs growing weaker by the minute, so that she
could scarcely believe they still supported her, and still
he looked at her with his vivid blue eyes bright and
gleaming.

'I like Jem.'

She tried to steady her voice, but the effect of hard
masculine hands on her arms and the touch of his body
pressing her even closer almost undermined her self-
control. He bent his head and when he spoke in a low,
shiveringly deep voice, his breath was warm on her lips.
She half-closed her eyes instinctively as she looked up
at him, then immediately looked away again while
keeping her face upturned.

'I like the little guy too,' he whispered, brushing his
lips on hers. 'But right this minute I prefer little girls,
beautiful little girls with dark silk hair and gold in
their eyes.' He kissed her lightly and smiled. 'One
particular girl with gold in her eyes.'

'Scott——' she began.

'Hmm?'

He slid his hands around behind her head and twined
his fingers in the silky softness of her hair, pulling back
her head still further until he gazed down at the invitation of her slightly parted lips with a curious little half-

smile. His thumbs pressing gently to the curve of her cheeks, he kissed her with a thoroughness that took her breath away, and Fern clung to him with her hands pressed hard against his back.

With a soft, deep murmur of sound he pressed his mouth to the vulnerable softness of her neck and throat, and the dark fringe of her closed eyes, before once more seeking her mouth. His arms seemed to possess an unbelievable strength as he bound her to him, and it seemed to Fern that her feet must have left the ground, for she felt sure she must be drowning in the sheer excitement of his kiss.

Big brown hands cradled her face when she opened her eyes again, and she looked into the vivid blueness of his with a dazed certainty about only one thing— she could never marry Roy, no matter what persuasion he brought to bear. Scott was smiling, in a way that brought warmth to his eyes and crinkled his tanned face in a way that was almost unbearably familiar, and she responded without being fully aware that she was doing so.

He went on looking at her for several seconds before he slowly shook his head. 'What are you going to say to him, Fern?'

For a moment Fern could only try to recapture her self-possession as she fought against an incredible chaos of emotions that chased one another through her head much too rapidly to make any kind of sense. Then she scanned the brown face that looked down at her with such intensity, and shook her head. 'Roy?'

The way in which he put her away from him, so gently but firmly, suggested he knew that only when she was no longer in contact with him could she bring her senses to order, but she felt strangely bereft without him. Retrieving his cigarette from the ashtray, he drew on it while he walked back to stand once more by the

mantel with an arm along its length, then he expelled
the smoke in a long blue curl from his lips. He looked
across at her, and Fern detected a ghost of his usual
smile touch his mouth for a moment.

'I'd find it kind of awkward in his shoes, honey, if
I'd asked a girl to marry me and she said no. Working
in the same office makes for a kind of—intimacy, doesn't
it? Will he be satisfied to have you go on being his
secretary when he wants you to be his wife?' He ran
a hand through his thick hair and laughed shortly.
'Hell, I know I wouldn't!'

It was something Fern hadn't thought about before,
and her expression told him as much. She thought
about it for a moment now, then shrugged helplessly
and spread her hands in appeal. 'I hadn't thought
about it, Scott, I just hadn't thought about it from that
angle.'

Somehow she had expected him to come up with
some kind of a solution, and she was disappointed
when he said nothing but merely stood by the mantel
smoking his cigarette, as if it was something that did
not concern him, his eyes narrowed very slightly. It
seemed such an alien situation to Fern, and she felt
completely at a loss for the moment. She had never
been in the position before of telling her employer
that she would not marry him, and she could not
imagine how she was going to do it.

Nor did she see how she was going to go on working
for Roy in the circumstances, not in the same way she
had until now. She had very definitely made up her
mind that she was not going to marry him, but how she
was going to tell him so was a different matter, for it
involved so much more than just an emotional liaison;
it was her job too.

Walking back to where she had left her coffee cup,
she bent and picked it up, realised it was empty and

put it down again. 'Would you like more coffee, honey?' he asked.

His speaking almost startled her, and she shook her head instinctively. 'No; no, thank you, Scott.' Looking at her wristwatch was automatic too, and he eased himself away from the mantel when she made the gesture as if he knew what she was going to say next. 'I ought to go, I've got quite a lot to do this morning, things I should have done yesterday.' Perhaps the brief hesitation before she moved to actually go was to give him time to persuade her not to, but in any case he said nothing to try and change her mind, but followed her when she walked to the door.

Reaching round her, he opened the door, letting in the light and the warm September air with its dusty cereal smell from the barley field, and she felt the great lurch her heart gave when his body touched hers for a moment before he drew back. She had come to join him so lightheartedly, but somehow the mood had completely changed in the short time she had been with him, and she regretted it bitterly.

It seemed to have changed after he had kissed her, and she could not believe he regretted it so much that he was now so ready for her to go without a word to try and persuade her to stay with him. She turned in the doorway and found him so close behind her that she instinctively put her hands to his chest to prevent a collision. In a moment his arms were around her and pulling her close until she could feel the steely strength of him as if it was taking over her own more malleable softness and moulding it inextricably to his body.

She yielded up her mouth to his kiss without hesitation, and he put a hand to the back of her head, holding her firm while he kissed her, and letting her go only when it seemed to Fern that she would never breathe again. She clung to him for a moment longer, her senses unaware of anything but his nearness and the urgency of her need for him, and quite unconscious of the car that had come down the track from the house, slowed for a moment while she was hugged close to Scott, then gathered speed rapidly and raced on down the rest of the way to the road with erratic fury.

Scott smiled down into her face, lightly kissing the very tip of her nose. 'Go and do your housework, honey-girl,' he told her in a voice warmed with laughter. 'I need to think!'

'Scott——'

She did not know what she wanted to say, only that she did not want to leave the strong, exciting closeness of his arms, but another, much harder kiss silenced her objection and he eased her out of his arms, holding her at arm's length with his hands at her waist.

'Just give me time to get things straightened out first, honey, then I'll have time to *really* concentrate on you!'

Something lurking deep in his eyes brought a flush to her cheeks and a sudden leaping urgency to her heartbeat as she closed her fingers around the strong brown wrists and held them for a moment so that he could not withdraw his hold on her. 'Straighten out your sister's—affairs?' she ventured, and Scott nodded, his mouth tightening for a brief moment.

'I have to do it, Fern, even if I am chasing shadows— will you bear with me?'

'Yes, of course.' Her own situation was brought home to her then, and she looked up into his face and frowned. 'Scott, what shall I say to Roy?'

For a moment he said nothing, then he half-smiled and she thought there was an edge of bitterness on his voice. 'Why not tell him the truth, sweetheart? After all, being who he is, he knows all about plain speaking— just tell him that you can't marry him because you don't love him.' He bent his head swiftly and kissed her mouth. 'And don't let that soft heart of yours change your mind, huh?'

Fern had heard Scott leave his cottage early the next morning, and wondered where he could be off to so early in the day; it was a question that kept recurring in her thoughts all day while she worked; she wished he had confided in her. Obviously he was pursuing something to do with his half-sister's ill-fated romance, but he had said nothing to her about his intentions and the fact was more hurtful than she would have believed possible. She had thought he trusted her.

Most of her work was up to date and she was sitting gazing rather absently out of the window into the garden when Roy came in a few minutes before she was due to leave for the day. It was the first time she had seen him that day, and she thought he seemed a little less effusive than usual, although he smiled at the sight of her as he always did, and came across to her desk.

When he rested his hands on her desk and leaned across the way he did, it meant he was going to kiss her and, knowing that, Fern managed to get up out of her chair before he actually did so, though she could imagine how he frowned at being frustrated. He watched her walk over to the filing cabinet with some letters and she could sense his dislike.

'Fern?'

After a second or two he followed her, standing immediately behind her while she filed the letters in her hand, and making it impossible for her to turn without coming into contact with him. Pressing back against the cabinet as far away as she could get from him, she tried to pass, but there was nothing she could do about the sudden pressure of his body holding her where she was.

'What is it, my love?'

Fern did not look at him; she felt curiously guilty somehow just standing there, knowing she was going to tell him that she had made up her mind not to marry him, even though she had no reason to feel as she did. 'I've been thinking over what you asked me, Roy.' The tip of her tongue flicked nervously across her lips and she tried to step around him, only to be brought up by his stepping aside to block her escape.

He was watching her with an intensity she could feel without having to see his face or his eyes. 'And?'

He knew her answer, that was clear from the tone of his voice. It had a harsh, rasping edge there was no mistaking, and Fern wished he need not take it so badly, knowing at the same time that it was just the way Roy would take anything he did not like. This time she made more of an effort and managed to get past him and back to her desk, though he followed her and stood once more leaning on his hands while he watched her steadily.

'I can't marry you, Roy. I'm sorry, I realise I'm probably being a complete idiot, but I—well, I just can't, that's all. I'm sorry.'

Roy said nothing for a moment, but Fern could feel the tension in him as if they were in bodily contact, and she felt oddly shivery somehow. 'I saw you, Fern.' She looked up and frowned, and saw that his usually friendly brown eyes had a gleam as hard as agate. 'When you were coming out of Redman's cottage yesterday morning, after telling me you had—what was it?— a lot to do in the house! I saw you kissing him, Fern! Or should I have said he was kissing you? Which was it, Fern?'

Stung to her own defence and refusing to feel guilty

about anything that had happened between herself and Scott, she looked up at him and met his eyes squarely. 'Both, perhaps,' she told him, slightly breathless with anger. 'I didn't know you'd been watching me, Roy!'

'Damn it,' Roy swore, 'I was driving past and I couldn't do anything else but see you! You were right there on the doorstep of his cottage for the whole world to see, if they cared to!'

'I'm sorry.'

Heaven knew why she was apologising to him, except that she suspected at least some of the anger he showed was caused by hurt, and she felt sorry about that. Roy turned away after a moment or two, one hand running despairingly through his hair as he walked over to his own desk, then he turned and looked across at her once more before he flopped wearily on to the edge of his desk, as if he felt suddenly too tired to stand any longer.

'Oh God, Fern, don't you realise that you're wasting your time mooning over somebody like Scott Redman? He's not the type to do other than love 'em and leave 'em; he's a drifter, a cocky Romeo who collects women like some men collect stamps! You won't pin him down, ever—even you!'

It was a bitter, angry tirade and it aroused Fern to Scott's defence as nothing else could have done, though he probably did not realise it until it was too late. She faced him across the big room and the gold flecks in her eyes sparked like flashes of fire as she stuck out her chin in defiance of his opinion.

'Nor is he the type to push a little boy aside to get his own way,' she told him in a low breathless voice. 'You helped me decide when you were so ready to send Jem away if I didn't want him around! Did you really think I'd marry you on those terms, Roy? Did you really think I'd stand for Jem being—thrust aside as if he was a piece of property to be disposed of as convenient?'

For several moments Roy said nothing, but sat with his hands rolled tightly and his good-looking face set with anger. Then he got to his feet and stood tall and stiff, his hands thrust into the pockets of his trousers, almost as if it was the only way he could keep from striking out. He did not look directly at her, she noticed, but at some point above her head, and his brown eyes were hard and unforgiving.

'It seems I had a lot of wrong ideas about you, Fern. In the circumstances I can understand that you don't want to go on working for me—or with me. I'm sorry, but it would be impossible, of course, I see that.'

'Yes, of course.'

She moved about packing up the things on her desk automatically and without conscious effort. Then picking up her handbag she walked over to the door, turning to look back at him where he stood watching her with eyes that had a curiously blank look and with his mouth firm and tight and quite unforgiving. Yet somehow it was that tight, prim look that made her certain at last that it had not been Roy whom Faye de Hahn had loved so desperately.

'I'm sorry, Roy—goodnight.'

'Goodnight!'

She hesitated a second longer, then turned and hurried out, closing the door behind her. She was almost at the end of the long track home before it suddenly dawned on her that she had been dismissed from her job, and the realisation made her catch her breath for a moment. Her cottage in the country, her pleasant job, living next door to Scott had all depended on Roy, and she had put it all in jeopardy by being too outspoken; by defending Scott Redman so fervently when Roy belittled him.

The cottage had never looked so good to her before as she walked down the central path between her garden and Scott's, and seeing the blank empty look of his windows and the closed door was somehow the last straw. He must be still out, for there was no sign of him at all, and as she put her key in the door and let herself in tears ran down her cheeks—tears of self-pity, she was the first to admit, but harrowing for all that, and there seemed nothing she could do to stop them.

It was getting quite late when she heard Scott come home, and she wished she had more strength of mind than to peep out from behind her kitchen curtain when she heard the sound of his car and his back door closing shortly afterwards. He was bound to have seen her and, knowing Scott, he was just as certain to come in and see her.

She·had stopped weeping for herself and her misfortune by then, but there were still traces of redness around her eyes, and a trembling unsteadiness about her mouth when she attempted to smile a greeting. She stood back and let him in, only minutes after he arrived, and he looked at her as he came inside, pulling a wry face but saying nothing until they walked through into the little sitting-room.

'What's wrong, honey?' he wanted to know.

It was just like Scott to come straight to the point, she thought, and felt weepy again suddenly when she remembered that she was soon to move away, and would probably never see him again. Making some effort to appear normal, Fern invited him to sit down, then made to turn back into the kitchen.

'Would you like some coffee?' she asked. 'Have you had a meal?'

'Yes, to both questions,' he told her with a grin, then

came over and took her arm instead of sitting down as
she asked him to. He turned her round to face him,
holding her in front of him and looking down at her
for a second or two before he said anything more. 'And
you haven't told me what's wrong.' He tilted her chin
on one hand and raised her face to him; his eyes sweeping over her features slowly and coming to rest on the
tell-tale eyelids. 'You've been crying, honey-girl; who's
upset you?'

'No one, I just——' It had to happen, Fern thought
despairingly as she started to cry again, and Scott was
shaking his head at her. 'I've got the sack, Scott! I've
lost my job!'

'Good God, I don't believe it!' He gazed down at her
tearful face in disbelief, while Fern did her best to
assert her normal self-control. 'Honey, do you mean to
tell me that because you said you wouldn't marry the
guy, he fired you right there and then?'

Fern brushed a hand across her eyes and shrugged
unhappily. 'Not exactly for that,' she confessed.

'For what, then?'

'I said——'

She found it wasn't at all easy to explain, especially
when she remembered that what had annoyed Roy as
much as anything else she said was her fervent defence
of Scott. But misunderstanding her sudden choking
off her words, Scott drew her into his arms and held her
tightly, one hand on the back of her head, her face
pressed to his chest while he stroked her hair gently.

'Oh, Fern honey, what have you been up to while
I've been gone, eh?'

Her voice was muffled, but Fern did her best to explain; omitting nothing, not even her hasty and impulsive defence of him, and she felt the brief vibrance
of his laughter ripple through her just before he kissed
her forehead, and his voice was close to her ear.

'Oh, you little nut! Fancy getting yourself sacked for a kid you hardly know and the guy who lives next door! Are you crazy?'

A slight frown drew her brows together when she looked up at him, though she did nothing to break the firm and comforting hold he had on her. 'It isn't funny, Scott!'

Another light kiss brushed across her brow. 'No, I know it isn't, honey, but this time you really let your soft heart rule your head, didn't you?'

'Somebody had to make a gesture for Jem!' She met his eyes for a moment, then looked down again and shook her head. 'I thought *somebody* ought to.'

Scott was looking down at her, more serious suddenly, although his eyes had a vivid blueness that did strange and disturbing things to her senses when she met them briefly. Long fingers slid beneath her chin and lifted it and he half-smiled at her as he spoke. 'I think I have the answer to Jem's problems, honey, if things work out the way I hope they do—and I can't see any reason why they shouldn't.'

Fern was ready to be reassured, but she was completely at a loss at the moment to know what he meant. 'Scott, what are you talking about?'

He kissed her almost absently, and she slid her arms around him and hugged close, leaning back only far enough to see into his face while he explained. 'It was something you said about Jem being the first Lady Barton's son. I've talked to the guys in the pub in the village and I've never heard anything of a son, not a word. Another thing—Jem doesn't get treated like he was the heir to a place like Barton's Fen. And how come Roy stands to be the next in line if Sir James's Italian lady doesn't produce a family, if Sir James already has an heir?'

Slightly dazed by the speed of events, Fern frowned

at him curiously. 'Are you saying that Jem *isn't* Sir
James's son? That Roy lied about him?'

'No, no, no, honey; I'm saying that Lady Barton, the
first Lady Barton, died ten years ago, so Jem definitely
couldn't be hers. Now you think carefully, honey; exactly what did Roy say when he told you about Jem?
Did he say he belonged to the first Lady Barton?'

Fern was trying to think clearly and not finding it
easy. She frowned, then shook her head. 'No—no, he
didn't. He said—he said that Sir James was a widower
when he met his present wife, and he didn't want any
complications, meaning Jem, so he left him with Roy.'

'And you automatically assumed that he meant Jem
belonged to the first Lady Barton!'

'Well, yes, of course.' She shook her head, her heart
hammering hard suddenly as she looked up into Scott's
brown, wryly smiling face and the vivid blue gleam in
his eyes. 'But he can't be, can he, Scott?'

'No way!' He held her a little more firmly, his hands
tight on her bare arms. 'I've been to London to find
out for myself, honey; I should have thought of it before
instead of trying to sort through the local records. Your
Somerset House up there has a record of everybody that
ever was born, married or died for the past couple of
hundred years or so, and I found the answer there. Sir
James Barton is Jem's father all right, but the record
shows that a male child was born to Faye Beatrix de
Hahn nearly six years ago and that he was christened
James, after his father—Jem for short! And not here—
in Boston!'

'Oh, Scott!'

'Yeah!' He eased his hold at last and put her gently
away from him reaching into his pocket for one of the
long cigarettes he smoked and lighting it automatically
while he stood over near the fireplace. Looking across
at her, he smiled, a rather tight smile that missed out

those fascinating crinkles at the corners of his eyes. 'I knew there'd been a baby, but nobody round here seemed to know anything about it. Most simply remembered a girl that used to live here and who went away after a while. A stranger passing through; a foreigner.' He caught her eye and grinned ruefully. 'Like me and you, honey—here today and gone tomorrow!'

It was automatic to glance out of the window when he spoke, at the thick black darkness and the stillness; the wind was still and the rustling chestnut that sheltered the cottages made no sound. It was a wide, bare countryside with an air of secretiveness, and it had been so for too long to be disturbed by the passing through of the occasional stranger like her and Scott— or Faye de Hahn.

Fern shivered. 'I know what you mean,' she said.

Scott came back to her, holding her by her arms and looking down into her face once more. 'It was you put me on the right track, honey, when you said Sir James looked on Jem as a complication. A long and ancient line like the Bartons and a title at stake—can you imagine a man in his position thinking of his eldest— his *only* son so far, as a complication?'

'No, of course he wouldn't—I should have seen that too.' She kept her eyes on a spot immediately below his chin where a neat collar and tie replaced the more usual open neck. 'But I'm glad he isn't Roy's, Scott. I can't help being glad about that.'

Once more a long finger raised her face to him and he smiled down at her with a hint of mockery in his eyes. 'You haven't still got a soft spot for him, have you, honey? You're not going to change your mind and tell him you'll marry him after all?'

She thought he knew the answer to that well enough, and a swift, unexpected thrill of elation ran through her whole body as she stood within the circle of his arms. 'I told Roy I couldn't marry him and nothing's happened to make me change my mind, Scott. What's more, I don't somehow think I'll be given the chance to change it.'

Scott bent to kiss her mouth lightly, carelessly as he mostly did. 'Just give *him* half a chance, honey-girl, and he'd let you change your mind!'

'Scott, if you——'

'No, honey, no more heart-searching today! I've got things to do tomorrow, and I've had a heavy day, I need my sleep!' He kissed her once more, but this time for slightly longer and with more fervour, his mouth lingering warmly before he let her go, and there was a hint of the old mockery in his smile as he put her away from him. 'I'll see you tomorrow when I've slept for an hour or two! Goodnight, honey-girl, sleep tight!'

CHAPTER NINE

It seemed strange to be going back to work for Roy after the events of the past couple of days, but as it happened Fern saw very little of him. He had come to the office each morning and given her the necessary instructions for the day's work, then disappeared again for the rest of the day, showing his face again only briefly, when she was on the point of leaving.

He had said very little beyond the few words necessary to give her instructions, and to bid her goodnight when she left, and in a way Fern was thankful, for she was not at all sure that she would have known what to say to him in the circumstances. It seemed incredible that their situation could have changed so much in such a short time, but it was obviously the way Roy wanted it to happen.

She regretted the nature of their parting two days ago personally, but at the same time she felt it had been Roy rather than herself who was responsible for what bitterness there was and she saw no reason to blame herself. What concerned her more than Roy's attitude at the moment was the fact that Scott had gone off in his car the day following his revelations concerning his half-sister and Sir James Barton, and she had not seen him since.

He had told her no more than that he had things to do, and he had been much too mysterious for Fern's liking; the fact that he had been gone for two days now made matters worse. She would not have believed it, but she found it alarmingly lonely without him, and she wished he had felt able to confide in her further. It hurt too, for she had thought he trusted her completely with the knowledge of his sister's tragedy; instead he had been gone for a second whole day now and there was still no sign of him coming back.

She was finishing off the last of the day's work before going home, rather absent-minded in the circumstances, but aware that every so often Roy was eyeing her curiously, and had been ever since he came back to the office half an hour before. He was there for longer, too, than he had been the afternoon before, sorting through the paperwork she had put on his desk with a kind of vague aimlessness that suggested to Fern that he had something to say and did not quite know how to say it.

She was actually packing up to go home when he looked across at her for the umpteenth time in half an hour, and in this instance he caught her eye and made an attempt at a smile before getting up from his desk and coming across to her. He did not lean forward on his hands as he had always done in the past, but stood tall and straight and rather stiff, his eyes evasive once more.

Obviously he had something to say, and Fern suspected it was an attempt to do something about the coldly formal attitude he had maintained for the past couple of days. Seeing how difficult he seemed to be finding it, she felt rather sorry for him and smiled encouragingly when she looked up. He responded, though still with a certain reserve, she recognised.

'I'm sorry, Fern.' An apology was the last thing she expected, and Fern blinked at him uncertainly for a moment. 'I perhaps wasn't altogether fair, blaming you for something that probably wasn't your fault.'

She was anxious to have the atmosphere between them relieved, or she would have pointed out that she had nothing to blame herself for, but she smiled and shook her head. 'You don't have to apologise, Roy. You were quite right about the situation—it wouldn't work out if I stayed on, not as things are, and it's much better if I go. I don't blame you too much and—well, it's much the best thing.'

He still hovered, and it was clear he had something else in mind to say, but the anxious look in his brown eyes that she was so familiar with was, in this instance, qualified to some extent by a glint of resentment, and she knew he would never entirely forgive her, no matter how much regret he professed. He probably had not expected her to accept the situation as readily as she did either, and he was frowning over it.

'You still want to leave?'

Fern started to remind him that it had been his decision, not hers, but it seemed rather unimportant somehow at the moment, so she shook her head and let it pass. 'Oh yes, I think it's best, Roy. It's by far the easiest solution in the circumstances, don't you think?'

He hesitated for a moment, and she thought that once more she had not responded in the way he had expected. Then he shook his head and shrugged, and she again felt a twinge of pity for him, for he had created a situation he did not like but was helpless to do anything to change.

'Yes, of course it is,' he said. 'I'm sorry, Fern.'

Her inclination was to tell him that she was sorry too, but it was possible such a confession might be misconstrued, so she simply went on putting away her things and kept her eyes on what she was doing. 'Is there anything else you want me to do today?' she asked, and Roy shook his head. Picking up her handbag, Fern came around to the other side of the desk and paused, looking up at him. 'Then I'll go—goodnight, Roy.'

'Goodnight!' He was still standing there while she walked across the room, then he turned swiftly just as

she opened the door, a frown between his brows; but a
frown of uncertainty rather than anger. 'Fern!' She
looked across enquiringly, but stayed where she was
with a hand on the door handle, and after a second or
two he shook his head. 'Nothing. I'm sorry—it doesn't
matter.'

Fern wished he did not look quite so lonely and uncertain standing there, but there was absolutely nothing she could do about it, so she turned and closed the
door behind her, then started for home. Heaven knew
what he had had in mind to say, but she was frankly
relieved that he had changed his mind about saying it.

Once she was outside and making tracks for home,
Fern's thoughts switched immediately back to Scott and
whether or not he would be back tonight. She sincerely
hoped so, for apart from anything else, she had experienced such a sense of loss last night in the silent cottage
that she had no wish to repeat the experience tonight.
She had missed not only the comfort of knowing that
the next door cottage was occupied, but the additional
solace of knowing that it was Scott who was so close
at hand.

The windows in both cottages were so small that on
dull evenings, like today, the rooms became dark very
early and it was necessary to use artificial light long
before it would normally have been needed. The light
in Scott's cottage window caught her eye as she came
along the track and she smiled suddenly and quickened
her pace over the rough ground. Scott was home, and
she was more anxious and happy to see him than she
would have believed possible.

The immediate temptation was to call on him instead
of having her evening meal first, and while she was still
hesitating on the step with the key in her hand, his
door opened and the decision was taken from her by
Scott himself. Opening his door wide, he stood for a

moment looking at her in silence with a deep glowing
warmth in his eyes that stirred her senses to alarming
response. Then his brown face creased into the familiar
grin and he winked.

'Hi, duchess!'

'Hello.' Fern fought desperately to control her emotions, but they responded to him in a way she could
do nothing about, and her heart was beating so hard
that it almost deafened her. 'I thought you'd gone back
to Canada without telling me,' she said, in a voice she
tried hard to keep steady. 'You've been gone two days!'

He stood there in the shadowy doorway with the artificial light behind him giving a bright golden fairness
to his hair, and Fern realised just how reproachful she
must have sounded when he shook his head at her. A
hint of a smile still hovered about his mouth and she
did not look at his eyes because she found them much
too disturbing in the present situation.

'Did you miss me?' he asked, soft-voiced.

'I was—curious.'

She made the admission rather than answer him
truthfully about whether or not she had missed him;
she thought he knew that quite well without her assur-
ances. His laughter was inevitable, she knew that too,
but somehow it hurt more than she would have believed. Then, almost as if he realised it suddenly, he
stopped laughing and reached out a hand for her, drawing her with him into his cottage, and holding her
hands tightly in his so that there was no hope of her
resisting, even had she been inclined to.

'Are you in desperate need of your dinner, or have
you got time to listen to me for a while?' he asked, and
Fern looked up at him in such a way that he must have
known the answer even before she gave it.

'I'm dying to know what you've been doing,' she confessed, and let herself be drawn into the circle of his

arms without protest, while he looked down at her with a ghost of the familiar grin. She met his eyes for a moment and made no pretence of hiding what she felt about his apparent lack of trust. 'I presume it had something to do with Faye, in which case I don't know why you didn't trust me enough to tell me where you've been and what you were going to do next. You——'

His mouth over hers stopped the rest of her protest and Scott was smiling when he looked into her eyes. 'I'm sorry, honey, but I like to get things sorted out before I confide in anybody—even you. Although I'm sure you're the positive soul of discretion!'

'Scott, don't tease me!'

He shook his head and smiled, then led her to an armchair, perching on the arm of hers rather than take the other chair, with an arm resting lightly across her shoulders while he talked. It was so good being close to him again that the first few words he said went right beyond her comprehension, for she was headily aware of the vigorous strength of him and of the mingled masculine scents of after-shave and the tobacco of those long cigarettes he smoked.

'Anyway, I think I have Jem's future solved, honey.' The blue eyes smiled down at her when she glanced up quickly. 'I thought that would bring you out of your day-dream,' he laughed. 'Are you listening to me, Fern, or am I wasting my time?'

'No, of course you're not. Please, Scott, I really am *very* interested.' She could hardly tell him that he was the cause of her distraction, and she made a determined effort to concentrate when the arm across her shoulders gave her a brief hug and he bent to drop a kiss on the top of her head.

'Then I'll tell you about my travels!'

'Where *have* you been?' she asked. 'Up to London again?'

'There, and for part of the time I was in Italy.'

Fern stared at him, unable to grasp the gist of what he was saying for a moment, although her heart was hammering urgently fast for some reason she could not yet decide. 'Italy? You've been in Italy?' Then it began to come to her and she turned in her chair so that she could look up directly into his face, her eyes bright with anticipation. 'You've been to try and find Sir James! Oh, Scott, tell me, please! Don't keep me in suspense— what happened?'

He seemed to have sobered suddenly and her eyes followed him when he got up from the arm of her chair and walked across to take a cigarette from the box on the mantel, lighting it before he said anything else. Almost as if he needed time to think, Fern thought dazedly.

He turned and looked at her at last, blowing smoke from between pursed lips, and she could only guess at what was in his eyes. 'I saw Sir James; it wasn't too hard to get in to see him, even though he knew who I was. You'd have thought he'd have avoided anyone to do with Faye like the plague, wouldn't you?' There was such bitterness in his voice that Fern shuddered.

'What did he say to you?'

'He admitted he was Jem's father and that Faye had been his—girl-friend.' He hated giving her any other name, Fern realised, and sympathised with his feelings. 'He didn't even seem to think he needed an excuse for acting the way he did. According to him, he never had any intention of marrying Faye, and he says she knew it.' He shrugged and she thought he was trying not to recognise that his sister could have been living in a fool's paradise when she wrote about getting married. 'Whatever the rights and wrongs of that, I figure he has a bit of a conscience about Jem, and that's how come he wasn't put in to a home or an orphanage.'

'But he didn't want him with him?'

'Oh no, and having seen the present Lady Barton I can see his point to some extent—she looks like a real fireball.' He laughed shortly and drew on his cigarette before he went on. 'What it boils down to is that he's quite happy to let him go to anyone who's willing to take him on, and the outcome is that I'm to get legal custody, with a possibility of adopting later—the lawyers will fix it.'

'Does Roy know?' she asked.

He glanced at her, sharply she thought, but the question had been impulsive. 'I guess so by now,' he said. 'Sir James was going to ring him tonight.'

'Oh, Scott, it's wonderful! I'm so glad, for Jem's sake.'

Scott smiled, although it was not his usual open, uninhibited smile. 'Yeah, I figure Jem will be pleased, which is what matters most.'

'Oh, but of course he will be! You've always got on so well together, you and Jem, so much better than he did with Roy. I don't think Roy likes children very much.'

'But you do, eh, honey?' She nodded and was dismayed to realise that she had coloured furiously. Scott was looking at her steadily from his place beside the old-fashioned fireplace, and he seemed curiously preoccupied for the moment. 'I think the kid will like Canada; it's a good place to grow up in, and he'll have everything he wants, his grandmother'll see to that!'

'Oh, I'm sure he'll love it!'

'We'll be leaving in about four weeks, all being well,' he went on.

'He'll be so excited!'

She was on her feet, unable to contain her excitement, and her hands were pressed tightly together while she considered all the advantages Jem would have living with a doting grandmother and an uncle who would see that he soon forgot his lonely early years. But then something else struck her, and it was as if she had been hit by a physical blow. She no longer smiled, but stared across at Scott with all the shocked surprise she felt showing clearly in her eyes.

'You're—you're going back to Canada in four weeks?'

His smile had a touch of unusual gentleness, and his voice too seemed to touch every nerve in her body with its quiet firmness. 'That's right, honey, it's my home.'

Fern coped with a sudden rising panic, and she tried to find reasons and excuses. 'But I thought you liked it here, Scott.'

She was desperate for him to stay, she realised a little wildly. Even though she would soon be leaving Thorpe St Mary herself; if he could at least have stayed in England—— She shook her head to dismiss the kind of thoughts that ran chaotically through her brain, and recalled what Roy's opinion had been.

He had seen Scott as a man who collected women as some men collect stamps—but she was convinced Roy was wrong. She wouldn't believe it of him; she didn't want to believe it, but realising why she felt the way she did stunned her almost as much as the initial announcement of his departure had done. His smile was unbelievably gentle and did nothing at all to help her, but made her feel suddenly very small and vulnerable.

'Didn't you realise I'd be going home as soon as I'd settled this business of Faye's, honey?'

He sounded so much as if he was offering consolation, and the thought of him being able to read what she had unwittingly betrayed made her suddenly self-conscious. His sympathy was something she shrank from, and yet she seemed unable to do anything about her blankly unhappy look. Then he reached out an arm and curled his long brown fingers invitingly, calling her over to him.

'I don't dislike it here, honey, and the past couple of months have been more fun than I could have dreamed they would be in the circumstances, thanks to you. But you must have known I'd be going home as soon as all this was over.'

'Yes. Yes, I suppose I did.' She wished she could stop her voice from trembling, but with Scott's strong right arm about her, and his voice so deep and disturbingly soft, it wasn't an easy fact to accept, and her voice betrayed how she felt. 'I just hadn't thought about it—of you going so soon.' Keeping her eyes on his firm and slightly crooked mouth, she wished she had the strength of will to ease herself from his embrace, to evade the long fingers that curved about her slim waist. 'When will you be going, Scott? Will it really be in only four weeks?'

'It all depends on how things work out, honey. I have things to settle, like making travel arrangements for us, and letting my folks in Canada know that there'll be new blood arriving. They'll want to lay on a party for sure!'

'Are there many of you?' She showed interest automatically, to give herself something else to think about apart from the inescapable fact that he would be gone in a matter of weeks.

'Cousins from Pop's side of the family, and mine, both lots of grandparents; we're a close family and he'll get quite a welcome!'

Fern felt dismayingly tearful, for she realised more and more every minute that she was losing not only her cottage and her job, but Scott too, and it was the loss of Scott that made her most unhappy. It was something she could not think about without wanting to cry like a baby and pleading with him to stay.

Her voice was small and unsteady and the arm about her waist somehow made things even harder to bear. 'I—I expect he'll get spoiled, won't he?'

'Spoiled rotten,' Scott agreed cheerfully. 'But he'll survive it—I did!'

'And you'll be happy to be back home.'

'Of course I will, honey.'

'You won't—miss anything? I mean, you haven't become attached to Thorpe St Mary—or anything?'

He followed her meaning easily enough, as he was bound to, she realised despairingly, and he lifted her chin on one long finger and looked down into her face for a moment before he answered. 'Sure I will, honey-girl. I'll miss the sunsets,' he kissed her mouth lightly each time he ticked off his list of things he would miss most, 'and the open spaces, the rain and the blustering wind off the sea. Most of all I'll miss having a gorgeous little brunette with gold in her eyes to argue with and make coffee for; but I'll still be happy to be home.'

Her legs felt almost too weak to hold her as she stood in the circle of his arm, but she was too unhappy to look up at him, even to appreciate his vow that he would miss her most of all. 'I'll be looking for somewhere else to live and to work,' she said. 'I've got about four weeks to go too, less now, I suppose, but we might go about the same time.'

He drew her closer into the curve of his arm and she was pressed to the hard unyielding length of him, her heart beating fast when she looked up and saw the familiar gleam of laughter; hurt because he could laugh when she felt so unhappy. 'I think you could be right, honey.' He brushed his lips across her brow and smiled. 'But first I'd like you to hold my hand when I do a little job for the Reverend.'

Distracted for a moment from her unhappiness, Fern looked up at him curiously. 'Mr Maybury?'

'Uh-huh!' He hugged her close. 'Like I got conned into opening the local church fête,' he told her, and obviously minded a lot less than he professed to. 'By some mischance the Rev discovered who I was and pinned me down to opening his village fair in my capacity as visiting celebrity, but I'll be a whole lot happier if you're there to hold my hand, honey-girl. Will you?'

'Yes, of course, but——'

She was utterly confused, and from his laughter it was obvious he realised it and found it amusing. He dropped a light kiss on her brow and put both arms around her, holding her close to the steely strength of him, the bright warmth in his eyes reviving her sagging spirits remarkably.

'I didn't know you were a celebrity, Scott.'

'I expected you to tumble to it before now,' Scott confessed with a shake of his head for her apparent slowness. 'Like I expected you to know I wouldn't like leaving you behind when I go home.'

'Scott!'

She stared at him with the conviction that she had not heard him say what he did. But he was still talking about her not recognising his identity and ignored her surprise. 'I guess it's all to do with the different accent or dialect, or whatever. The Rev had the advantage because he saw it written. You see, my publisher over here made the mistake of addressing a letter with my professional name and the mail man passed on the information to the rector. To do the Rev justice, he did put clamps on the mail man making it public knowledge, under pain of hell and damnation or something equally bloodcurdling, but he made the most of it for his own ends.'

'Scott——'

'Mind you, I wouldn't have thought with the kind of

thing I write I was the ideal man for a church fête, but as the price of his keeping quiet about me for the rest of my stay here, I promised I'd cut the ribbon at the opening of the church fête, and crown the Harvest Queen, but I don't think I'd have the nerve to do it on my own.'

Dazed, but squirming with impatience, Fern frowned at him. 'Scott, what do you mean—the kind of thing you write? What *do* you write? And if you say "this and that" as you always do when I ask you, I'll——'

'You'll what, sweetheart?'

It was breathtaking to notice how easily he used the endearment, and he was laughing, with his face only inches above hers so that the warmth of his words breathed with shivering softness against her lips. Then his arms tightened suddenly, and the laughter in his eyes became something much more exciting and harder to meet, making her head spin.

She seemed bound to him inescapably and it was instinctive to put her arms around his neck as his mouth came down to hers. It was a kiss like no other kiss she had known, and she yielded her very heart to the excitement of it, willingly complying with the demands of the strong arms that held her, coaxing her to respond, and the commanding, pleading urgency of his mouth, until her whole body shuddered with helpless ecstasy.

And when he left her mouth for the soft, vulnerable warmth of her throat and neck, she closed her eyes in a glow of incredible pleasure, whispering his name over and over. It seemed like an eternity before he raised his head, and the look she saw in his eyes brought a swift urgency to her pulse, catching at her breath and making her evade his gaze for a few seconds while she buried her head against his chest.

'Fern?' A big gentle hand stroked her hair, and she

lifted her face to look at him again. The blue eyes had
a bright gleaming look that set her heart racing and
she smiled like a woman in love, because that was what
she readily admitted she was. 'Will you come back with
me, sweetheart?'

'To Canada?'

He nodded. 'With me and Jem.'

There was nothing to consider really, and she knew
it, for she would have gone with him willingly, wher-
ever and whyever he wanted her to, but the temptation
to tease him with a taste of his own medicine was just
too much to resist. 'First of all I'd like to know who
I'll be travelling with if I decide to go to the other side
of the world,' she told him, and Scott pulled her close
again and kissed her hard.

'Will it make any difference, sweetheart? Will you
only come with me if I meet with certain specifica-
tions?'

'No, of course not!' It wouldn't, she was quite sure
of it, but she looked up at him in mingled excitement
and pleading. 'But please will you stop teasing me,
Scott, and tell me who you are?'

'How about Alec de Hahn?' he asked, and Fern
stared at him.

She had heard the name so many times before, as
most people must have done, but never pronounced
with a short 'a' before, as he had done when he told
her about his stepfather and half-sister. Only the addi-
tion of that particular first name made her realise why
he had expected her to recognise who he was before,
and she shook her head dazedly.

'*The* Alec de Hahn?'

She gave the name a long 'a' as she was more used to
thinking of it, and Scott smiled recognition of the English version. 'Pop always said his folks used a long "a"!'
he confessed, 'but over there it's got to be Han instead

of Harn. Whichever you call it, that's it. I took Pop's name when I started to write because he gave me a lot of encouragement, and I knew him for a lot longer than I knew my own father.'

'And he didn't mind?'

He knew what she meant and Fern wished at once that she hadn't made her surprise so obvious. Alec de Hahn wrote the kind of books that not only made fortunes, but also earned the author a reputation for a certain earthiness of style, and she could not yet realise that it was the same man who now held her in his arms.

'No, honey, he didn't mind.'

She was thinking about Faye, and the letters appealing for help. Scott had said his stepfather had pushed them to the back of a drawer and not even let him see them—in his righteous, puritan soul, as Scott had described it, he had cut his daughter out of their lives, and that was not the kind of man Fern thought would approve of seeing his name on the kind of books Alec de Hahn wrote—the kind of books that Scott wrote.

'I was thinking of——'

'I know, sweetheart.' He kissed her gently and looked down at her for a second before he shook his head. 'You didn't know him, Fern; Pop was a strange mixture. He was very puritan about women, about his own women especially, they must be—good. Hell, no, that isn't the word I want!'

'Caesar's wife?' Fern suggested softly, and he smiled ruefully.

'Above reproach,' he agreed. 'I guess it's pretty old-fashioned and maybe a bit unfair, but it was Pop; it was the way he was, and as long as you went along with him he was a real fine man. He just found it too hard to forgive, I guess, though I've often thought during the past year that maybe he wanted to, if only he'd known how.' He looked at her once more and his eyes were darkly sober. 'He didn't mind the books I wrote, sweetheart—do you?'

'No, of course not, I've read several of them. I'm just—dazed, that's all.' She looked up, asking for his understanding. 'I just hadn't thought of you being anyone as—well, as well known, Scott.' She blinked at him uncertainly. 'You *are* Scott, aren't you?'

He cradled her in his arms with her face upturned, then he kissed her mouth for long enough to make her breathless and light-headed, a smile making the familiar web of lines about his eyes. 'I'm Scott, my love. Scott Alexander Redman, if you can believe it; just the same as always but with a little more in the bank than you figured, that's all. Do you have anything against successful men?'

Fern shook her head. There was nothing about him that she could think could change her mind about loving him as she did, and she reached up to put her arms around his neck again, looking at him with the warm gold flecks in her eyes dancing with happiness. 'Not against this particular man,' she told him softly. 'I think I'd love you even if you proved to be Bluebeard himself—I can't help myself.'

'And I love you, my sweetheart. I didn't realise how much until it came to the point of thinking about leaving and going home; I don't know what I'd have done if you'd said you wouldn't come with me.'

Her eyes gentle with laughter, Fern looked up at him through her lashes. 'I haven't actually said I'll come back with you yet,' she reminded him.

Scott's hold tightened and he sought her mouth determinedly, kissing her until she was breathless and starry-eyed, and she clung to him as if she would never let him go. 'Why don't we fix it so the Rev marries us before we go, eh? Then I'll be sure you come with me.'

'Here? In Thorpe St Mary?'

'Any reason why not?' Scott demanded, and she shook her head, willing enough to be persuaded. 'Will you marry me, honey-girl? Will you let me sweep you off your feet and carry you off to *my* wide open spaces —will you, sweetheart?'

'I'd love it!' Fern told him breathlessly, and would have said more, but she was given no opportunity.

Harlequin
Announces the
COLLECTION
EDITIONS
OF 1978

Harlequin's Collection 12
ANDREA BLAKE
Night of the Hurrica

Harlequin's Collection 106   1.25
ANNE WEALE
If This Is Love

stories of special
beauty and significance

25 Beautiful stories of parti

In 1976 we introduced the first 100 Ha
— a selection of titles chosen from ou
the past 20 years. This series, a trip down memory lane,
proved how great romantic fiction can be timeless and
appealing from generation to generation. Perhaps
because the theme of love and romance is eternal, and,
when placed in the hands of talented, creative, authors
whose true gift lies in their ability to write from the heart,
the stories reach a special level of brilliance that the
passage of time cannot dim. Like a treasured heirloom,
an antique of superb craftsmanship, a beautiful gift from
someone loved, — these stories too, have a special
significance that transcends the ordinary.

Here's your 1978 Harlequin Collection Editions . . .

...quin 1978 Collection Editions . . .

124 Lady In Harley Street
Anne Vinton
(#985)

126 Will You Surrender?
Joyce Dingwell
(#1179)

(#983)

123 Island In The Dawn
Averil Ives
(#984)

125 Play The Tune Softly
Amanda Doyle
(#1116)

Original Harlequin Romance numbers in brackets

ORDER FORM—Harlequin Reader Service

In U.S.A.:
MPO Box 707,
Niagara Falls, N.Y. 14302

In Canada:
649 Ontario St., Stratford,
Ontario N5A 6W2

Please send me the following Harlequin Collection novels. I am
enclosing my check or money order for $1.25 for each novel
ordered, plus 25¢ to cover postage and handling.

☐ 102   ☐ 107   ☐ 112   ☐ 117   ☐ 122
☐ 103   ☐ 108   ☐ 113   ☐ 118   ☐ 123
☐ 104   ☐ 109   ☐ 114   ☐ 119   ☐ 124
☐ 105   ☐ 110   ☐ 115   ☐ 120   ☐ 125
☐ 106   ☐ 111   ☐ 116   ☐ 121   ☐ 126

Number of novels checked _____ @ $1.25 each = $ _____

N.Y. and N.J. residents add appropriate sales tax $ _____

Postage and handling $ .25

                                          TOTAL $ _____

NAME _____
                (Please print)
ADDRESS _____

CITY _____

STATE/PROV. _____ ZIP/POSTAL CODE _____

ROM 2178

Offer expires December 31, 1978